HIGH CRIME AREA

HIGH CRIME AREA

TALES OF DARKNESS AND DREAD

JOYCE CAROL OATES

The Mysterious Press

an imprint of Grove/Atlantic, Inc.

New York

Published simultaneously in Canada
Printed in the United States of America

FIRST EDITION

ISBN: 978-0-8021-2265-0
eBook ISBN: 978-0-8021-9213-4

The Mysterious Press
an imprint of Grove/Atlantic, Inc.
154 West 14th Street
New York, NY 10011

Distributed by Publishers Group West

www.groveatlantic.com

14 15 16   10 9 8 7 6 5 4 3 2 1

To Richard Burgin

Contents

The Home at Craigmillnar

Early shift is 6:30 A.M. which was when I arrived at the elder care facility at Eau Claire where I have been an orderly for two years. Maybe thirty minutes after that, when the elderly nun's body was discovered in her bed.

In fact I'd gotten to work a few minutes before my shift began as I usually do, in nasty weather especially (as it was that morning: pelting-rain, dark-as-night, first week of November), out of a concern for being late. For jobs are not easy to come by, in our economy. And in Oybwa County, Wisconsin, where I have lived all my life except for three and a half years "deployed" in Iraq as a medical worker. I am a conscientious orderly, with a very good reputation at the facility.

If I am interviewed by the county medical examiner I will explain to him: it is a wrongly phrased description—*Body discovered in bed.* For when I entered Sister Mary Alphonsus's room in Unit D, my assumption was that the Sister was alive, and the "discovery" was that she was not alive, or in any case not obviously alive. I did not "discover" a "body" in the bed but was shocked

1

to see Sister Mary Alphonsus unmoving, and unbreathing, with a gauzy fabric like muslin wrapped around her head (like a nun's veil or wimple), so that her face was obscured.

She was unresponsive to me. Yet even at this, I did not "discover" a "body"—it was natural for me to believe that the elderly woman might have lapsed into a coma.

(Not that death is so unusual in an elder care facility like ours—hardly! All of our patients die, eventually; Unit E is our hospice wing. But the death of the resident in room twenty-two of Unit D was not expected so soon.)

In my Iraqi deployment my instinct for things *not-right* became very sharp. Out-of-ordinary situations there might arise— suddenly—as in a nightmare—an explosion that could tear off your legs. You had to be alert—and yet, how is it possible to be always alert?—it is not possible. And so, you develop a kind of sixth sense.

And so as soon as I entered the room after knocking—twice— at the door—I saw that things were *not-right,* and the hairs at the nape of my neck stirred. There was no light in the room and Sister Mary Alphonsus was still in bed—this was *not-right.* For Sister Mary Alphonsus was always "up" before the early shift arrived, as if pride demanded it. The nun was one of those older persons in our care who *does not accept that she is elderly,* and will turn nasty with you if you behave as if she is.

Sister?—in a lowered and respectful voice I spoke. Always I addressed Sister Mary Alphonsus with courtesy, for the old woman was easily offended by a wrong intonation of voice.

Like a bloodhound keen for scent, this one was sharp to detect mockery where there was none.

Not a good sign, Sister Mary Alphonsus wasn't yet awake. Very strange, the light above her bed hadn't been switched on.

And a strong smell of urine in the room. Unexpected, in Sister Mary Alphonsus's room, whose occupant wasn't incontinent, and who was usually fussy about cleanliness.

When I switched on the overhead light the fluorescent bulb flickered like an eye blinking open.

The shock of it, then: seeing the elderly nun in her bed only a few feet away, on her back, not-moving; and wrapped around her head some sort of gauzy white fabric like a curtain, so her face was hidden. And inside the gauze the Sister's eyes shut, or open—you could not tell.

Died in her sleep. Cardiac arrest.

By the time of our senior consulting physician's arrival at the facility, at about 9 A.M., it was clear that elderly Sister Mary Alphonsus was not likely in a coma, but had died. The strip of gauzy material had been unwound from the woman's head by the first nurse who'd arrived at the bedside, and dropped heedlessly onto the floor.

I am not a "medic": I am an "orderly." In all medical matters orderlies defer to the medical staff. I had not tried to revive Sister Mary Alphonsus nor even to unwind the cloth from her head, which did not appear to be tightly tied. So far as I knew, the patient might have been alive following a stroke or heart attack.

A legal pronouncement of death can only be made by a physician.

In a senior care facility like ours, Death strikes suddenly, often overnight. Often, within an hour. Cardiac arrest, pulmonary embolism, stroke—like strikes of lightning. If an elderly resident becomes seriously ill, with pneumonia for instance, or is stricken with cancer, he or she is transported to Eau Claire General for specialized treatment; but most of our residents have long-standing medical conditions, of which the most insidious is *old age*.

In the matter of Death, when a living body becomes "dead," there are legal procedures that must be followed. Our senior consultant was required to sign the death certificate and the county medical examiner's office had to be informed. If the deceased had listed next of kin in her file, this individual or individuals would now be notified and arrangements would be made for removal of the body from the facility and for burial.

About this, I knew nothing, and would know very little—though I would learn, inadvertently, that the elderly nun had died *intestate*.

(*Intestate*: a fancy word for dying without a will! A kind of nasty ring to this word *intestate,* makes you think of *testicles,* worse yet in this facility of old men *testicular cancer.* Not a welcome thought.)

Next time I came into contact with Sister Mary Alphonsus was after Dr. Bromwalder's examination, when the body was covered with a white sheet. With another orderly, I lifted it onto a gurney to push quickly and as unobtrusively as possible to the facility's morgue in the basement—*Man, she heavy for an old lady!*

I couldn't resist peeking under the sheet: Sister Mary Alphonsus's face was mottled red, a coarse-skinned face you could not have identified as female. The thin-lashed eyes were shut and the mouth that had resembled a pike's wide mouth in life hung loosely open.

She anybody you knew, Francis?

No.

There'd never been any doubt in Dr. Bromwalder's mind that the eighty-four-year-old woman had died of cardiac arrest, in her sleep. She'd been a cardiac patient: she'd had a chronic condition. It had not seemed to be life threatening, but all signs suggested heart failure and not a stroke; under these circumstances, an autopsy was not warranted.

The gauze wrapped around the nun's head was certainly too flimsy to have caused suffocation. It had seemed to the senior consulting physician but mildly mysterious—"eccentric"—but many "eccentric" things happen in elder care facilities, among patients who may be mentally as well as physically ill, and so not much was made of the gauzy fabric except by some of the nursing staff of Unit D, who were puzzled, curious—*Why would the woman do such a thing? What does it mean?*

The fabric was believed to have been taken out of the Sister's belongings, some of which were kept in a small bureau in the room. It did appear to be a curtain, or part of a curtain—white, dotted-swiss, somewhat soiled, a cheap material.

Maybe she was confused, in her sleep. Wrapped a curtain around her head thinking it was a nun's wimple!

Maybe she knew she was dying. It was some kind of religious thing, like after a Catholic confesses her sins to a priest—penance?

Among the staff of Unit D, Sister Mary Alphonsus had not been a favorite. To her face the nurses called her *Sister,* behind her back *the old nun.*

Or, *the old nun who'd run that terrible orphanage at Craigmillnar.*

It would be noted that Sister Mary Alphonsus was discovered to be unresponsive in her bed by the Unit D orderly, Francis Gough, who'd immediately notified the nursing staff. Time: 7:08 A.M.

Less certainly, it was determined that Sister Mary Alphonsus had died several hours earlier—Dr. Bromwalder's estimate was between 3 A.M. and 6 A.M. This was a reasonable estimate judging by the temperature of the corpse when it was first examined by the doctor, in the absence of a pathologist. In the pitch-black of the early morning, hours before dawn, patients are most likely to "pass away" for these are the hours of Death.

There was a death here today. Old woman in her eighties, in my unit. She was found dead in her bed—died in her sleep they think.

Oh Francis! That's so sad. I hope it wasn't you who found her.

It's OK, Mom. It wasn't me.

Most mornings when the early staff began their rounds we would find Sister Mary Alphonsus fully awake and sitting in the chair beside her bed, a blanket over her knees, and a missal opened in her hands, though after near-seventy years of the Catholic missal, you would not think that the nun required an actual book to help her with prayers; or, Sister might have her rosary of wooden beads twined in her fingers, as she waited for an orderly to help her into her wheelchair. Her gaze would be vacant until you appeared—and like a raptor's eyes the vague old-woman eyes would come sharply into focus.

If you greeted her with a friendly smile—*Good morning, Sister!* —she was likely to frown, and to make no reply, as if you'd disturbed her in prayer, or in some private and precious drift of her mind. And so I'd learned to say nothing to her, much of the time. What would be rude behavior with other patients had come to seem, to me, expected behavior with Sister Mary Alphonsus.

Sister Mary Alphonsus was one of those residents at Eau Claire who ate meals in the patients' dining hall, not one whose meals were brought to her room. Despite the difficulty involved in delivering her to the dining hall, which was sometimes considerable, depending upon her medical ailment of the moment, Sister Mary Alphonsus insisted upon this.

In her former life, before "retirement," she'd been a prominent figure in her religious order—for more than two decades, director of the Craigmillnar Home for Children. This was a Catholic-run orphanage about sixteen miles north and east of Eau Claire, at its fullest occupancy containing more than three hundred children.

In the dining hall, Sister Mary Alphonsus asked to be seated at a table with several elderly women whom she might have considered "friends"—of whom two were, like herself, retired Sisters of Charity of St. Vincent de Paul who'd also been at Craigmillnar.

You would think that the Sisters of Charity would speak of their shared past at Craigmillnar, but they hardly spoke at all except to comment on the food. Like elderly sisters who'd seen too much of one another over the decades, and who had come to dislike one another, yet clung together out of a fear of loneliness.

Though it was difficult to imagine Sister Mary Alphonsus as one susceptible to *loneliness*.

Few relatives came to visit the elderly nuns. They'd had no children—that was their mistake. Beyond a certain age, an elderly resident will receive visits only from her (adult) children and, if she's fortunate, grandchildren. Others of their generation have died out, or are committed to health-care facilities themselves. So virtually no one came to see these elderly nuns, who with other Catholic residents of the facility attended mass together once a week in the chapel.

Their priest, too, was elderly. Very few young men were entering the priesthood any longer, as even fewer young women were entering convents.

Though I'm not Catholic often I observed the mass from the rear of the little chapel. "Father Cullough"—(who made no effort to learn the nuns' names)—recited the mass in a harried and put-upon voice, in record time—scarcely thirty minutes. The mass used to be said in Latin, as I know from having seen old prayer books in my family, that had been published in Scotland

and brought to this country; now, the mass is said in English, and sounds like a story for simple-minded children.

In the front row of the chapel the elderly nuns tried to keep awake. Even Sister Mary Alphonsus, the sharpest-witted of these, was likely to nod off during the familiar recitation. When the priest gave communion, however, at the altar rail, the old women's tongues lapped eagerly at the little white wafer, the size of a quarter. My gaze shifted sharply aside, for this was not a pretty sight.

Once, when I was wheeling Sister Mary Alphonsus back to her room after mass, the wheelchair caught in a ridge of carpet in the floor, and Sister Mary Alphonsus was jostled in her seat, and lashed out at me—*Clumsy! Watch what you're doing.*

Sister, sorry.

You did that on purpose didn't you! I know your kind.

Sister, I did not. Sorry.

You will be sorry! I will report you.

Many of the patients threaten to report us, often for trivial reasons. We are trained not to argue with them and to defer politely to them as much as possible.

Think I don't know YOU. I know YOU.

Yes, Sister.

"Yes, Sister"—(the elderly woman's croaking voice rose in mockery)—*we will see about that!*

I made no reply. My heart might have leapt with a thrill of sheer dislike of the old woman, but I would never have said anything to goad her further. It was said of the former Mother

Superior at Craigmillnar, by the nurses' aides who were obliged to take intimate care of her aged body—*Bad enough she has to live with herself. That's punishment enough.*

Yet by the time Sister Mary Alphonsus was back in her room, her interest in reporting me to my supervisor had usually faded. She'd been distracted by someone or something else, that annoyed or offended her. She'd have forgotten Francis Gough entirely, as one of little worth.

Not that she knew my name: she did not. While others called me *Francis,* Sister Mary Alphonsus could barely manage to mutter, with a look of disdain—*You.*

She did know the names of the medical staffers, to a degree. She knew Dr. Bromwalder. She knew Head Nurse Claire McGuinn, if but to quarrel with her.

A care facility like a hospital is a hierarchy. At the top are physicians—"consultants." Nurse-practitioners, nurses and nurses' aides, orderlies—these are the staff. An orderly is at hand to help with strenuous tasks like lifting and maneuvering patients, including patients' lifeless bodies; changing beds, taking away soiled laundry, washing laundry; pushing food-carts, and taking away the debris of mealtimes; sweeping and mopping floors; taking trash outside to the Dumpsters. (Trash is carefully deployed: there is ordinary waste, and there is "clinical waste.") My original training (at age nineteen) was on-the-job at Racine Medical Center plus a week-long course in "restraint and control."

There were few violent patients at Eau Claire but I was well prepared for any I might be called upon to "restrain and control."

You need two other orderlies at least if you need to force a patient onto the floor. How it's done is you force him down onto his stomach, an orderly gripping each arm, and an orderly securing the legs. It's going to be a struggle most times—even the old and feeble will put up a considerable fight, in such a situation; the danger is in getting kicked. (When you're the most recently hired you are assigned the legs.) In this position—which looks cruel when observed—the patient's back is relatively free so he can breathe, and he's prevented from injuring himself.

Unlike cops who are allowed "pain" as an element in restraint-and-control, medical workers are not allowed "pain" and may be legally censured if patients are injured.

Despite my training, there have been injuries of patients I'd been obliged to restrain and control, both in U.S. care facilities and in the medical units in Iraq.

None of these were my fault. And yet, there were injuries.

The nurses were gossiping: Sister Mary Alphonsus had no close next of kin.

Or, if there were relatives of the deceased woman, they were distant relatives who had no wish to come forward to identify themselves.

Maybe no wish to associate themselves with the individual who'd been director of the Craigmillnar Home for Children, that had been shut down in 1977 by Oybwa County health authorities and the State of Wisconsin.

Just recently too, Craigmillnar was back in the headlines.

A full week after her death on November 11, no one from the Oybwa County medical examiner had contacted the facility. So it appeared, Dr. Bromwalder's death certificate had not been questioned.

The gauzy strip of "curtain"—unless it was some kind of nun's "veil" or "wimple"—had disappeared from the premises. All of Sister Mary Alphonsus's things had been packed up and removed from room twenty-two and a new, unsuspecting arrival, also an elderly woman, had been moved in.

Yet, the subject of the mysterious "head covering" continued to come up, in Unit D. It seemed strange to me—(I said so)—that I appeared to be the only person to have seen Sister Mary Alphonsus fix something like a "head-shroud" over her head several times in the past. Some kind of cloth—might've been a towel—(I didn't remember it as white)—she'd drawn like a hood over her head, for whatever reason. I hadn't asked the Sister what she was doing of course. She'd have been offended at such *familiarity*.

One day our young consulting physician Dr. Godai asked me about this, for he'd overheard some of us talking.

So you'd seen the Sister putting some kind of "cloth" on her head, or around her head, Francis? When was this, d'you remember?

Might've been a few weeks ago, doctor. Maybe two months.

How often did you see the Sister putting this "cloth" on her head?

Maybe three times, doctor. I never thought anything of it, you know how old people are sometimes.

Dr. Godai laughed. He was the newest consultant on our staff, from the University of Minnesota Medical School. He had a burnished-skinned Paki look, dark-eyed, sharp-witted. Knowing that certain of the elderly patients and certain of the medical staff did not feel comfortable with him, as non-white, Dr. Godai was what you'd call forceful-friendly, engaging you with his startling-white eyes and smile sharp as a knife-blade. Between Dr. Godai and me there flashed a kind of understanding as if the elderly nun was in the room with us, helpless, yet furious, glaring at us in disdain and in hurt, that she could not lash out at us to punish.

Eccentric is the word, Francis. A kindly word. For you wouldn't want to say demented, deranged, senile—eh?

Dr. Godai and I laughed together. I wasn't naïve enough to think that Dr. Godai could ever be my friend, though we are about the same age.

I told Dr. Godai that each time I'd seen Sister Mary Alphonsus behaving in this way, putting a "shroud" on her head, I'd made no comment of course. I didn't even ask her if she was cold, or needed an extra blanket. Nor did Sister Mary Alphonsus encourage conversation with me or with others on the staff. In my memory it had seemed to me that the woman was just slightly embarrassed, and annoyed, by my having seen her with the "cloths." And so out of courtesy I turned away from her, as if I hadn't seen.

It's a strange life isn't it, Francis?—I mean, the religious orders. Poverty, chastity, service, obedience these nuns swore to.

To this, I made no reply. Dr. Godai was speaking bemusedly, and may have been thinking out loud.

Of course, I don't understand the Catholics, maybe. Are you Catholic, Francis?

No, Dr. Godai. I am not.

You are an arrogant young man. I will report you.

I know YOU. YOU will not get away with this.

There are two categories of geriatric patient. Those who persist in behaving as if they aren't elderly; or as if their current condition, inability to walk, for instance, is a temporary one; individuals who shuffle slowly, in obvious pain, leaning against walls, against the backs of chairs, out of pride. And there are those who have conceded that they are not "one hundred percent," but must use a cane, a walker, a wheelchair. (It's possible to think that a wheelchair isn't really "permanent"—it is always expedient, helpful more for the staff.) Each step you think is temporary and you will soon return to your real self, but that's not how it goes.

Sister Mary Alphonsus had been in the second category. She may have been elderly but not *old-elderly*; and she would resent bitterly your behaving as if she were. Her hearing, like her vision, was impaired, but Sister Mary Alphonsus was more likely to blame you for not speaking clearly, or loud enough, than she would blame herself. In fact, Sister Mary Alphonsus would never blame herself.

If she spilled food, or dropped something, and you were present—somehow, the fault lay with *you*. At first I'd thought this was a sign of dementia but later I came to realize, it was the woman's perception of *what is:* blame must be assigned, only just not with her.

Unlike most of the elderly women in the facility, Sister Mary Alphonsus hadn't been what you'd call frail. Her body was thick, waistless; her skin was leathery; her eyes were suspicious and close-set; her legs remained heavy, especially her thighs, that strained against the polyester stretch-pants she sometimes wore. Her most characteristic expression was a peevish frown.

Sometimes, Sister Mary Alphonsus seemed annoyed by rain outside her window, as if it had been sent to provoke *her*. For there was a small courtyard into which we could wheel patients, in good weather.

Once, I'd wheeled Sister Mary Alphonsus outside into this courtyard and had to go away on an errand, and by the time I returned it was raining hard, and Sister Mary Alphonsus had managed to wheel herself beneath an overhang, by an effort of both hands.

You did that on purpose! You are mocking me.

No one considered that it might have been poison that Sister Mary Alphonsus had taken. *Poison* that was her own soul.

It was general knowledge in Eau Claire: in recent months the children's home at Craigmillnar, that had acquired a "controversial" reputation since it had been shut down by state health authorities in 1977, had re-surfaced in the news.

Now, interest in Craigmillnar was part of a broad investigation into Catholic-run charity homes, hospitals, and organizations following a flood of disclosures of sexual misconduct by priests in the United States, with the complicity of the Catholic hierarchy. A militant group of former residents of the home at Craigmillnar, that called itself Survivors of Craigmillnar, had been picketing the archbishop's residence in Milwaukee, demanding acknowledgment of what they charged had been "widespread neglect and abuse" at Craigmillnar. The state attorney general was considering criminal charges against some former staff members who, the former residents claimed, had been responsible for a number of deaths at Craigmillnar in the 1950s and 1960s.

At the very least, the Survivors were demanding financial settlements, and a public apology from the Catholic Church.

Public apology!—my father laughed, bitterly. *The Church will apologize when Hell freezes over.*

Both my mother's and my father's families had been Catholic—they'd emigrated to Wisconsin from Glasgow in the 1920s—but no longer. My father and his older brother Denis had expressed disgust with the Church for as long as I could remember and when I was asked my religion on a form I checked *None.*

In Scotland there are many Catholics. People think that Scotland is all Protestant—this is not so. But lately, since the scandals of the pedophile priests and cover-ups by the Church, there has been a drop in the number of Catholics in Scotland, as in Ireland.

When allegations of abuse and negligence were first made against the Craigmillnar nuns, the diocese had defended the Sisters of Charity. There were Church-retained lawyers, threats of counter-charges. The archbishop, who'd been a bishop in Boston at the time of Craigmillnar's worst abuses, had issued a public statement regretting the "unprofessionalism" of the orphanage, but absolving his predecessor-archbishop, now deceased, from any blame associated with its administration. It was leaked to the media that church officials believed that the Craigmillnar Sisters of Charity were "not representative" of the Order; that there'd been in fact a "very small minority" of Sisters of Charity of St. Vincent de Paul who'd been involved in this "unprofessional" behavior. Those nuns still living had been "retired" from the Order.

In the Eau Claire elder care facility such subjects were not usually discussed. At least not openly.

The former lives of our patients are not our concern unless our patients want to talk about them, as sometimes they do; for it's important to some of the elderly that their caretakers have some sense of who they once were. For most of them, showing photos of grandchildren and boasting of careers will suffice.

Sister Mary Alphonsus, who'd been a resident at Eau Claire for the past eight years, had never spoken of her former life as Mother Superior at Craigmillnar—of course. Some time before I'd come to Eau Claire to work as an orderly, there'd been a coalition of investigators who'd sought to interview the elderly nuns in the facility, predominantly Sister Mary Alphonsus, but an attorney hired by the diocese had rebuffed their efforts with the argument that the nuns had long been retired, and were not in good health.

In 1997, in the wake of the slow-smoldering scandal, the name of the nuns' order was legally changed from the Sisters of Charity of St. Vincent de Paul to the Daughters of Charity of St. Vincent de Paul.

Still, there was a lingering wonderment not only in Unit D but elsewhere in the facility, regarding the sudden death of the former Mother Superior of the Craigmillnar Home for Children. As if the staff didn't want to surrender their most notorious resident quite so quickly.

Maybe (some were saying) Sister Mary Alphonsus had had a hand in her own death.

Since there'd been no autopsy. You could conjecture such things, that were not likely to be disproven.

(For what did Dr. Bromwalder know, or care? The senior consultant's hours at Eau Claire were the very minimum, if not less.)

Managed somehow to cease breathing. And her heart to cease beating.

The gauzy soiled "veil" or "wimple" wound around her head, hiding her face, had to be deliberate—didn't it?

Could be, Sister Mary Alphonsus felt remorse. For the children she'd had a hand in torturing and letting die of disease.

Could be, Sister Mary Alphonsus's death was a penance.

Put herself out of her misery?

Speculations wafted about me. But I was too busy working—pushing trolleys, gurneys, wheelchairs—sweeping and mopping floors, disinfecting toilets, hauling away trash to the Dumpsters out back—to be distracted.

Honorably discharged from the U.S. Army with the rank of corporal when I was twenty-six, four years ago this January.

Because of my training I'd been assigned to the medical unit. The work was tiring but exciting, always unpredictable. You were made to feel *For the grace of God, this could be me.* It makes you humble, and grateful. It's a feeling that will never fade. The first time a soldier died in my arms it happened in a way to leave me stunned, I could not talk about it for weeks. I have never talked about it even with my father. I'd thought *Is this what it is? Dying? So easy?*

There is nothing so precious as life, you come to know. First-hand you know this. And a sick feeling, a feeling of rage, that some people treat the lives of others so carelessly, or worse.

My first work back in the States was in Racine where I trained; my second job was Balsam Lake Nursing Home twenty miles north of St. Croix where my family lives. My third job has been here at the Eau Claire elder care facility where I am currently employed.

When we were growing up my father never spoke of his own childhood. I knew that he'd had a younger brother—who would have been one of my uncles—who'd died when he was a child. But I didn't know anything more.

Anything *of the past* was forbidden. We did not ask but we did not think to ask. My mother had warned us—*Your father isn't a man for looking back. That can be a good thing.*

Francis! Come home this weekend, Denis and I have to speak with you.

It was a weeknight in early November. At this time, Sister Mary Alphonsus had not yet passed away in her sleep.

Such urgency in my father's voice I had never heard before, not even when I'd left for Iraq.

In an exalted mood my father and my uncle Denis brought me with them to the Sign of the Ram which was their favorite pub, to a booth at the rear of the taproom behind the high-pitched din of the TV above the bar. Leaning our elbows on the scarred table, hunching inward. My father and my uncle Denis on one side of the table, and me on the other.

I felt a mounting unease. The thrill of such intimacy with my father and my uncle was *not-right*.

In fierce lowered voices they revealed to me their long-kept secret, that no one else knew: not my mother, and not my aunt who was Denis's wife. Not anyone in the family at the present time for those who'd known had died, and had taken their knowledge of the secret with them, in shame.

Here was the situation. My father spoke, and my uncle interrupted to complete his sentences. Then, my father interrupted. Then, my uncle. These are not men accustomed to speaking in such a way in lowered voices and with an air of commingled shame and rage. For it seemed, articles in the local papers had stirred in them memories of Craigmillnar. TV interviews with "survivors" of the home whose faces were blurred to protect their identities. One night Denis had called his brother during one of these interviews on the local station—*Jesus God, I think I know who that is. And you do, too.*

As boys, Denis, Douglas, and their young brother Patrick had been committed to the Craigmillnar Home for Children. Their father had died in an accident at the St. Croix stone quarry when he was thirty-three. Their mother, only twenty-six when Patrick was born, had had a mental breakdown and could no longer take care of herself and her sons; she began to drink heavily, she fed medications to the boys "to keep them from crying," she died in 1951 of a drug overdose. One day an uncle came for them to take them to the orphanage saying there was "no place" for them now—but he would come to get them again soon, in a few months perhaps. In time for Christmas, he'd promised.

Christmas 1951! It would be Christmas 1957 by the time they were freed of Craigmillnar, and their little brother Patrick dead.

In raw indignant voices the men said to me: God damn these jokes about nuns, stupid TV shows about nuns, on TV a nun is meant to be a comic figure but in life there was nothing funny about these women. They were like Nazis—they followed orders. What the Mother Superior instructed them, they fulfilled. Some of them were like beasts, mentally impaired. The convent had done that to them, you had to surmise. There was a kind of madness in them—you could see it in their eyes, that were always darting about, seeking out disobedience. The Mother Superior had been the cruelest. For the woman had been intelligent, you could see. And her intelligence had all turned to hatred, and to evil.

How the Sisters groveled, like all in the Church when confronted with a superior! The ordinary nun groveled to her Superior, the Mother Superior groveled to the Bishop, the Bishop to the Archbishop, and to the Cardinal, and to the Pope—a vast staircase, you are meant to think, ascending to God the Father.

It was strange, when you thought about it—years later. That the orphanage at Craigmillnar had been theirs to "administer." By the standards of the present day, was any one of the nuns qualified for such work? Did the director—this woman identified as Sister Mary Alphonsus—have any training in such administration? Were the "nurse-nuns" trained nurses? Were the "teacher-nuns" trained teachers? Had any of the nuns been educated beyond high school? (That is, parochial high school taught by nuns.) Very likely, many of the Sisters of Charity at Craigmillnar had barely graduated from middle school.

The brothers had vowed to protect Patrick, who was so small, and always terrified. Yet, at Craigmillnar, at once the brothers were separated and made to sleep in separate dormitories according to age.

The orphanage was overcrowded, drafty and dirty. Often two children shared a single narrow bed. You were—often—marched from one place to another through high-ceilinged corridors. There were mealtimes—school-times—prayer-times—bed-times.

There were "outdoor-times"—these were irregular, and brief. You were not allowed to speak except at certain times and then you dared not raise your voice. Laughter was rare, and likely to be a mistake. Prolonged coughing was a mistake. Sharp-nosed as bloodhounds the Sisters were alert to the smallest infractions of law. The Sisters could detect a squirming bad child amid a room of huddled children.

Most frantic were the Sisters about *bed-wetting*. The children were wakened several times a night to check their beds. Bed-wetters were singled out for terrible beatings, children as young as two and three. They were made to drape their soiled sheets around themselves and to stand in the cold for hours until they collapsed. You were punished for being unable to eat by being force-fed through feeding tubes wielded by the Sisters.

There were degrees of "discipline"—"punishment." One of them was "restraint"—the child's arms were bound by towels, tightly knotted, like a straitjacket. Circulation was cut off, there was likely to be swelling, and terrible pain. A child might be bound, water thrown over him or her, so that the binding was allowed to dry, and to shrink. (This had been done, more than once, to both Douglas and Denis. To this day, the men carried the physical memories of such punishments in their arthritic joints and jabs of pain in their muscles unpredictable as lightning-strikes.) There were beatings with the nuns' leather belts. There were beatings with pokers. There were slaps, blows with fists, kicks. Striking a child's head with a rolled-up newspaper—this was surprisingly painful. Husky shot-eyed Sister Mary Agatha beat children with a mop handle. Shut Patrick in a cupboard saying the "little devil" coughed and wheezed "for spite" and kept other children awake.

We were all beaten, we were made to go without proper food, we were made to sleep in cockroach-ridden beds, bedbug infestations and no one gave a damn. Neighbors in Craigmillnar must have known—something. The officials of the Church must have known. All those years! The Sisters of Charity could not have been so crude and so cruel at the start. The younger nuns—they were hardly more than girls—must have been shocked, and frightened. Just entering the convent—and being sent to Craigmillnar. Yet, at Craigmillnar, they became crude, cruel women. "Brides of Christ"—what a joke! Their Order of nuns was a service-order—service to the poor. Saint Alphonsus was one of their patron saints—he'd founded communities for the poor in slums in Rome. They'd vowed for themselves a life of sacrifice—celibacy, poverty, service, obedience. The catch was, the Sisters hadn't had to vow to love their charges, only to serve God through them. Soon then, they came to hate and despise their charges. A young child must be difficult to hate and despise, yet the Sisters of Craigmillnar hated and despised. They were quick to flare into anger, and into rage. They shouted, they screamed. They kicked and they struck us with rods. The teaching nuns struck us with the rods used to pull down maps over the blackboards. In their fury at our fear of them they threw pieces of chalk at us. They knocked us to the floor. They locked us in closets—"solitary confinement"—no food, and lying in our own shit. We did not know what we did wrong. There were crimes called "insolence"—"arrogance." A ten-year-old girl in the desk next to mine was struck in the face by our teacher, and her nose bled terribly. Her clothing was soaked in blood. She was forced then to remove her clothing, to stand naked and to wash her stained clothing in disinfectant. The bleach, the lye, was such that our hands burned. Our skins were so chafed, they bled easily. We worked in the kitchen, we helped serve up the maggoty food and we washed the dishes after meals in scalding water, with such meager soap, there were scarcely any bubbles. Everything was covered in a fine film of grease that could never be scrubbed away. We worked in the laundry, in the stinking lavatories we were made to clean the toilets and the floors. We cleaned the nuns' rooms and their stinking lavatories and bathrooms. Their stained tubs and toilets. We worked as grounds crews. We hauled trash, we mowed the rocky lawn. Denis ran away once, twice—how many times!—always brought back by county authorities, sometimes beaten, for he'd "resisted arrest." Douglas ran away once, and was brought back to the home in a police van, like a captured criminal.

We believed that we would die in the Home at Craigmillnar, as Patrick had died, and so many others. We had lost all hope of ever leaving. We were made to pray on our knees, on the bare floor—the prayer I remember was *Christ have mercy! Christ have mercy! Christ have mercy!*

It was a custom of the Craigmillnar staff to punish children for being ill by refusing to treat their illnesses or medical conditions—rheumatic heart, asthma, pneumonia, diabetes, influenza; contagious sicknesses like chicken pox, measles, and mumps, even diphtheria, swept through the drafty filthy dormitories. Catholic physician-consultants who were allegedly on the Craigmillnar staff failed to come to the home or, if they did, spent most of their time chatting with the Mother Superior and did not meet with sick children.

Children who died were often buried before their relatives were notified, in unmarked graves at the rear of St. Simon's churchyard a few miles away.

We never knew if any child had actually been killed outright, in the years we were there. There were rumors of such murders in the past. It was more likely a child might die of injuries eventually, or was let to die of illness. There were many "accidents"— falling down stairs, scalding yourself in the kitchen. Patrick was always hurting himself, and being "disciplined." He'd had asthma before Craigmillnar, that had not been treated. He got sick, he was never well but always coughing, puking. He coughed so hard, his ribs cracked. We begged the nuns to help him, to take him to a hospital, we thought that we could take him ourselves if we were allowed, we knew that pneumonia had to be treated with "oxygen" but the nuns laughed at us, and screamed at us to shut up. Mother Superior Mary Alphonsus knew of such things, and did not care. She had her own TV in her room. She ate well, she favored sweets. She had a heavy woolen coat and good leather boots for our terrible winters.

He died in January 1953. We had last seen him in the drafty, dank place called the Infirmary. He could scarcely breathe. There was a terrible wheezing in his lungs. It sounded like a wheezing of air from another part of the room—we kept looking up at the windows, that were so high, and ill-fitting. Patrick was shivering, yet his skin was burning-hot. His eyes were enormous in his face. His teeth chattered. He could not speak to us—he was too sick. Yet he clutched at us—his hands clutching ours.

He was let to die. They killed him. Asthma and pneumonia, poor Patrick couldn't breathe. Suffocated and none of them cared. And his body buried in the paupers' cemetery with the others.

They hadn't even let us know, when he died. A few days passed, before we were allowed to know.

In St. Simon's churchyard, the nuns and the priests of Craigmillnar are properly buried, with marble headstones. Facts of their birth-dates and death-dates are inscribed in stone. But the children's bodies, at the back of the cemetery—there are only little crosses to mark them, crowded together. Dozens of cheap little rotted-wood crosses, each at an angle in the earth. And Patrick, who would have been your youngest uncle, among them.

All their bones mixed together. As if their child-lives had been of no worth.

She had not commented, when the inquiries had first begun a few years ago. The pedophile priests had been protected by their Bishop, also. But investigators for the county and the state began listening to complaints and charges against the Craigmillnar

27

staff. A younger generation of prosecutors and health officials, taking the lead of investigators in other parts of the country. Journalists who weren't intimidated by the Church because they weren't Roman Catholics.

Yet, *she* held her ground. She hid behind a lawyer, the Church provided a lawyer to protect her, because of her position and rank. She had refused to give testimony. She had not been arrested, as some others had been in situations like hers. She'd been served a subpoena to speak before a grand jury in Oybwa County, but had suffered a "collapse"—and so had a medical excuse. With the excuse of being "elderly"—in her late seventies—the woman was spared further "harassment" by the state.

Journalists referred to Sister Mary Alphonsus as the "Angel of Death of Craigmillnar" since so many children had died in the home during her years as director: the estimate was as many as one hundred.

Sister Mary Alphonsus was reported to have asked: how one hundred was *too many*? They were poor children, from ignorant families, they'd been abandoned by their parents, or by their (unwed) mothers—they were the kind of children who made themselves sick, eating too much, stuffing their bellies, refusing to wash their hands, playing in filth, fighting with one another, falling down stairs, running outdoors—that they would get sick was hardly a surprise, yes and sometimes one of them died. Over twenty-six years it came out to only three or four a year who died, out of the 350 children at the Home: how was that *too many*?

In the Sign of the Ram we'd been drinking for more than two hours. The men's voices were low-pitched, trembling with rage. I had scarcely spoken except to murmur *My God* and *Yes.* For I was shocked and sickened by what the men had told me—and yet, not so surprised. As my mother would be shocked and sickened and yet—not so surprised. *Your father isn't a man for looking back.*

Leaving the pub with my father and my uncle seeing the men older than I'd recalled, each of them walking unsteadily as in fear of pain. And I realized I'd been seeing my father and my uncle walking this way, all of my life. Big men, men for whom the physical life is the primary life, men-who-don't-complain, men who laugh at discomfort, these were men who'd been deeply wounded as boys, the memory of pain in their tissues, joints, and bones, pain of which they would not ever speak, for to speak in such a way was to betray weakness, and a man does not ever betray weakness. And I felt a son's rage, and a sick fear that I would not be equal to this rage. For I thought *Why have they told me this? Why now?*

My car was at my parents' house. My father drove me back, with Denis. Wasn't I going to stay the night? my father asked. Laying his hand on my arm. And my mother too asked, wasn't I going to stay the night, my bed was all made up. Seeing in the men's flushed faces that something had been revealed, she could not share. I told them no, I wasn't staying. Not tonight. I had to get back to Eau Claire that night.

My father walked me back outside, to my car in the driveway. And he did not say *She is at that place you work—is she. She is in your "care."*

That November morning, the morning of the *discovery of the body,* I was the first of the early shift to arrive.

In the pitch-dark pelting rain making my way to the side-entrance of the facility. At this early hour the building was but partially lighted, with a warm look inside. No one? No one to see me? Quickly and stealthily I made my way to Unit D, that was near-deserted at this hour. Soon the facility would come awake: the nursing staff and the orderlies would begin their rounds, the patients would be "up" for their interminable day. But not just yet, for it was 5:46 A.M.

From a closet I removed a single pillowcase. In the pocket of my waterproof parka was a three-foot strip of gauzy curtain I'd found in a trash can. I'd snatched it out of the trash—not sure why. A smile had twisted my mouth—*What's this?* I thought I would find a purpose for it.

I have learned to trust such instincts. I have learned not to question my motives.

Quietly then I pushed open the door to Sister Mary Alphonsus's room which was at the end of a corridor. I did not breathe, my rubber-soled sneakers made no sound. Yet the elderly nun was part-awakened by my presence.

I shut the door behind me. Without hesitating, as if I'd practiced this maneuver many times, I stooped over her bed, gripped her shoulder with one hand to hold her still, with the other yanked the pillow out from beneath her head, and pressed it over her face. So swiftly and unerringly I'd moved, Sister Mary Alphonsus had no time to comprehend what was happening, still less to cry out for help. Now in the throes of death she struggled like a maddened animal, her fingers clawing at my wrists.

I was wearing gloves. Her nails would not lacerate my bare skin.

In this struggle of several minutes I crouched over the figure in the bed, the head and face obscured by the pillow. I was panting, my heart beat quickly but calmly. I did not utter a word.

I thought of my father Douglas, and of my uncle Denis. I thought of my uncle Patrick as a child, whom I had never seen. Buried in a pauper's grave, and his bones scattered and lost. But I did not speak. I did not accuse the evil woman, for what was there to say? You soon come to the end of speech as you come to the end of cultivated land, and stare out into the wilderness in which there are no names for things, as there are no familiar things. For what words would be adequate at this time, so long after the fact?—*God damn your soul to Hell. Disgusting old bitch, this is not the punishment you deserve.*

Her hands tried to grip my wrists, to push away the pillow. But her hands grew feeble. I smelled urine. I did not flinch. A pillow held tight over the face of an elderly cardiac patient will snuff out her life within minutes, if you do not flinch.

When I was sure that it was over, I removed the pillow. The pillowcase was soaked with the woman's saliva, tears. Her body that was surprisingly heavy, with a hard round stomach like an inverted bowl, lay limp and unresisting now. The face like a bulldog's face, contorted in death. I heard a harsh panting sound—my breathing. Hers had ceased, abruptly.

When death is only a matter of seconds, you think that it might be revoked. Life might be called back, if one had the skill.

But no. Once the match is shaken out, the flame is gone.

Without haste, with the precision of a veteran orderly, I removed the pillow from the soiled pillowcase, and pushed it snugly inside a fresh pillowcase. I took time to shake the pillow well down into the pillowcase. This action so frequently performed by me, in my role as orderly, like clockwork I executed it within seconds.

The bedclothes were badly rumpled, as if churned. These I tidied deftly, tucking in bedsheets as you learn to do in the U.S. Army as well.

There is pleasure in executing small perfect things. One, two, three—completed! On to the next.

(The soiled pillowcase I might have tossed into the laundry. No one would have thought to look for it there—for the death of the eighty-four-year-old nun would not be considered a "suspicious" death. Yet, I was cautious, taking time to fold the pillowcase neatly to slide it into my backpack, to be disposed of when I left work.)

I lifted Sister Mary Alphonsus's limp head, to wind the strip of cheap gauzy curtain around it, and to hide her flushed and contorted face. *Bride of Christ! Here is your wedding veil.*

Why did I take time to do this?—why, to risk suspicion where there would be no suspicion?

I've thought of it, often. But I don't know why.

A smile comes over my face at such times—a strange slow smile. Am I happy, is that why I am smiling? Or—is the smile involuntary, a kind of grimace?

I could not have explained any of this. Not even to my father. It seemed the "right" thing to do, at the time. It would be my secret forever.

"Dorothy Milgrum" had left no will, it would be revealed. And so, the deceased woman's modest estate would be appropriated by the State of Wisconsin.

How much did "Dorothy Milgrum" accumulate, in her years as chief administrator of Craigmillnar? It could not have been much. It was whispered among the staff that there was barely enough money for a decent headstone in the St. Simon's church-yard at Craigmillnar, where Sister Mary Alphonsus had secured a plot for herself years before.

I was the orderly charged with emptying, cleaning, and pre-paring the room for the next resident.

In the bureau in Sister Mary Alphonsus's room, amid her old-woman undergarments, stockings, and woolen socks, there was a packet of letters. I appropriated these, for there was no one to prevent me. It was a surprise to see so many handwritten letters, dated 1950s. Who'd written to the Mother Superior at Craigmillnar so often? And why had the Mother Superior kept these letters? The return address was Cincinnati, Ohio. The stationery was a pale rose color. The salutation was *Dear Dotty*. The signature was faded maroon ink—it looked like *Irene*. I tried to read a few lines, but could not decipher the curlycue handwriting. Another nun? A dear friend? There was also a packet of snapshots, yellow and curling. In these, Sister Mary Alphonsus was a young woman in her thirties—with sharp shining eyes, bulldog-face, wide glistening smile. She wore her nun's dark robes with a certain swagger, as a young priest might wear such attire. The wimple was tight around her face, dazzling-white. Her face looked cruelly and yet sensuously pinched, as in a vise.

In several snapshots the youthful Sister Mary Alphonsus was standing close beside another nun, a stocky broad-shouldered middle-aged woman with a moon-face and very white skin. Both women smiled radiantly at the camera. The older woman had flung off her nun's hood, her hair was close-cropped, gray. The older woman was taller than Sister Mary Alphonsus by an inch or so.

In the background was a lakeside scene—a rowboat at shore, fishing poles.

In the last of the snapshots the women were again standing close together, now both bare-headed, arms around each other's waist. These were thick arms and thick waists—these were husky women. Then I saw—it was a shock to see—that both women were barefoot in the grass, at the edge of a pebbly lakeside shore.

I thought—*They took these pictures with a time exposure. It was a new idea then.*

The snapshots and the letters covered in faded-maroon ink I burnt as I'd burnt the pillowcase soaked with a dead woman's saliva. If it had been in my power I would have burnt all trace of Sister Mary Alphonsus on this earth but the truth is, some smudge of the woman's sick soul will endure, multiplied how many hundreds of times, in the memories of others.

I would say nothing—not ever—to my father or to my uncle Denis but a certain long level look passed between us, a look of understanding, yet a look too of yearning, for what was concealed, that could not be revealed. When I next saw them, and the subject of the nun's death arose. My father had kept a newspaper to show me, the front-page headlines, though I didn't need to see the headlines, knowing what they were. In a hoarse voice Dad said—*Good riddance to bad rubbage.*

By which Dad meant *rubbish.* But I would not correct him.

Now that months have passed there is not much likelihood of a formal inquiry into the death of Sister Mary Alphonsus aka "Dorothy Milgrum." The Oybwa County medical examiner has never contacted us. Dr. Godai has left Eau Claire to return to Minneapolis, it has been announced. (Many, including me, were disappointed to hear that Dr. Godai is leaving us so soon though it isn't surprising that a vigorous young doctor like Dr. Godai would prefer to live and work in Minneapolis, and not Eau Claire.) Yet, I have prepared my statement for the medical examiner. I have not written out this statement, for such a statement might seem incriminating if written out, but I have memorized the opening.

Early shift is 6:30 A.M. which was when I arrived at the elder care facility at Eau Claire where I have been an orderly for two years. Maybe thirty minutes after that, when the elderly nun's body was discovered in her bed.

High

How much, she was asking.

For she knew: she was being exploited.

Her age. Her naïveté. Her uneasiness. Her good tasteful expensive clothes. Her *hat*.

Over her shimmering silver hair, a black cloche cashmere *hat*.

And it was the wrong part of town. For a woman like her.

How much she asked, and when she was told she understood that yes, she was being exploited. No other customers on this rainy weekday night in the vicinity of the boarded-up train depot would pay so much. She was being laughed-at. She was being eyed. She was being assessed. It was being gauged of her—*Could we take all her money, could we take her car keys and her car, would she dare to report us? Rich bitch.*

She knew. She suspected. She was very frightened but she was very excited. She thought *I am the person who is here, this must be me. I can do this.*

She paid. Never any doubt but that the silver-haired lady would pay.

And politely she said, for it was her nature to speak in such a way, after any transaction, *Thank you so much!*

Self-medicating, you might call it.

Though she hated the weakness implied in such a term —*medicating!*

She wasn't desperate. She wasn't a careless, reckless, or stupid woman. If she had a weakness it was *hope.*

I need to save myself. I don't want to die.

Her hair! Her hair had turned, not overnight, but over a period of several distraught months, a luminous silver that, falling to her shoulders, parted in the center of her head, caused strangers to stare after her.

Ever more beautiful she was becoming. Elegant, ethereal.

After his death she'd lost more than twenty pounds.

His death she carried with her. For it was precious to her. Yet awkward like an oversized package in her arms, she dared not set down anywhere.

Almost, you could see it—the bulky thing in her arms.

Almost, you wanted to flee from her—the bulky thing in her arms was a terrible sight.

I will do this, she said. *I will begin.*

She'd never been "high" in her life. She'd never smoked marijuana—which her classmates had called "pot," "grass," "dope." She'd been a good girl. She'd been a cautious girl. She'd been a reliable girl. In school she'd had many friends—the safe sort of friends. They hadn't been careless, reckless, or stupid, and they'd impressed their influential elders. They'd never gotten *high* and they had passed into adulthood successfully and now it was their time to begin *passing away.*

She thought *I will get high now. It will save me.*

The first time, she hadn't needed to leave her house. Her sister's younger daughter Kelsey came over with another girl and an older boy of about twenty, bony-faced, named Triste—(Agnes thought this was the name: "Triste")—who'd provided the marijuana.

Like this, they said. Hold the joint like this, inhale slowly, don't exhale too fast, *keep it in.*

They were edgy, loud-laughing. She had to suppose they were laughing at her.

But not mean-laughing. She didn't think so.

Just, the situation was *funny.* Kids their age, kids who smoked dope, weren't in school and weren't obsessing about the future, to them the lives of their elders just naturally seemed *funny.*

Kelsey wasn't Agnes's favorite niece. But the others—nieces, nephews—were away at college, or working.

Kelsey was the one who hadn't gone to college. Kelsey was the one who'd been in rehab for something much stronger than marijuana—OxyContin, maybe. And the girl's friends who'd been arrested for drug possession. Her sister had said *Kelsey has broken my heart. But I can't let her know.*

Agnes wasn't thinking of this. Agnes was thinking *I am a widow, my heart has been broken. But I am still alive.*

Whatever the transaction was, how much the dope had actually cost, Agnes was paying, handing over bills to Triste who grunted shoving them into his pocket. Agnes was feeling grateful, generous. Thinking how long had it been since young people had been in her house, how long even before her husband had died, how long since voices had been raised like this, and she'd heard laughter.

They'd seemed already high, entering her house. And soon there came another, older boy, in his mid-twenties perhaps, with a quasi-beard on his jutting jaws, in black T-shirt, much-laundered jeans, biker boots, forearms covered in lurid tattoos.

"Hi there Aggie. How's it goin!"

Agnes she explained. Her name was *Agnes*.

The boy stared at her. Not a boy but a man in his early thirties, in the costume of a boy. Slowly he smiled as if she'd said something witty. He'd pulled into her driveway in a rattly pickup.

"*Ag-nez.* Cool."

They'd told him about her, maybe. They felt sorry for her and were protective of her.

Her shoulder-length silvery hair, her soft-spoken manner. The expensive house, like something in a glossy magazine. That she was Kelsey's actual aunt, and a *widow*.

The acquisition of a "controlled substance"—other than prescription drugs—was a mystery to Agnes, though she understood that countless individuals, of all ages but primarily young, acquired these substances easily: marijuana, cocaine, amphetamines, OxyContin, Vicodin, even heroin and "meth."

Self-medicating had become nearly as common as aspirin. *Recreational drugs* began in middle school.

She was a university professor. She understood, if not in precise detail, the undergraduate culture of alcohol, drugs.

These were not university students, however. Though her niece Kelsey was enrolled in a community college.

Like this, Aunt Agnes.

It was sweet, they called her Aunt Agnes, following Kelsey's lead.

She liked being an *aunt*. She had not been a *mother*.

They passed the joint to her. With shaky fingers she held the stubby cigarette to her lips—drew the acrid smoke into her lungs—held her breath for as long as she could before coughing.

She'd never smoked tobacco. She'd been careful of her health. Her husband, too, had been careful of his health: he'd exercised, ate moderately, drank infrequently. He'd smoked, long ago—not for thirty years. But then, he'd been diagnosed with lung cancer and rapidly the cancer had metastasized and within a few months he was gone.

Gone was Agnes's way of explanation. *Dead* she could not force herself to think, let alone speak.

Kelsey was a good girl, Agnes was thinking. She'd had some trouble in high school but essentially, she was a good girl. After rehab she'd begun to take courses at the community college—computer science, communication skills. Agnes's sister had said that Kelsey was the smartest of her children, and yet—Silver piercings in her face glittered like mica. Her mouth was dark purple like mashed grapes. It was distracting to Agnes, how her niece's young breasts hung loose in a low-slung soft-jersey top thin as a camisole.

She brought the joint to her lips, that felt dry. Her mouth filled with smoke—her lungs.

He'd died of lung cancer. So unfair, he had not smoked in more than thirty years.

Yet, individuals who'd never smoked could get lung cancer, and could die of lung cancer. In this matter of life-and-death, the notion of *fair, unfair* was futile.

"Hey Auntie Agnes! How're you feelin?"

She said she was feeling a little strange. She said it was like wine—except different. She didn't feel *drunk*.

Auntie they were calling her. Affectionately, she wanted to think—not mockingly.

So strange, these young people in her house! And her husband didn't seem to be here.

Strange, every day that he wasn't here. That fact she could contemplate for long hours like staring at an enormous boulder that will never move.

Strange too, she remained. *She* had not died—had she?

There was her niece Kelsey and there was Kelsey's friend Randi, and bony-faced Triste, and—was it Mallory, with the tattoos? She wasn't sure. She was feeling warm, a suffusion of warmth in the region of her heart. She was laughing now, and cough-ing. Tears stung her eyes. Yet she was *not sad*. These were tears of happiness not sadness. She felt—expansive? elated? excited? Like walking across a narrow plank over an abyss.

If the plank were flat on the ground, you would not hesitate. You would smile, this crossing is so easy.

But if the plank is over an abyss, you feel panic. You can't stop yourself from looking down, into the abyss.

Don't look. Don't look. Don't look.

Her young friends were watching her, and laughing with her. A silvery-haired woman of some unfathomable age beyond sixty in elegant clothes, rings on her fingers, sucking at a joint like a middle school kid. *Funny!*

Or maybe, as they might say, *weird.*

How long the young people stayed in her house Agnes wouldn't know. They were playing music—they'd turned on Agnes's radio, and tuned it to an AM-rock station. The volume so high, Agnes felt the air vibrate. She had to resist the impulse to press her hands over her ears. Her young friends were laughing, rowdy. Kelsey was holding her hand and calling her *Auntie.* It was a TV comedy—brightly lit, and no shadows. Except she'd become sleepy suddenly. Barely able to walk, to climb the stairs, Kelsey and another girl had helped her. Someone's arm around her waist so hard it hurt.

"Hey Aunt Agnes, are you OK? Just lay down, you'll feel better."

Kelsey was embarrassed for her widow-aunt. Or maybe—Kelsey was amused.

She was crying now. Or, no—not crying so they could see.

She'd learned another kind of crying that was *inward, secret.*

Kelsey helped her lie on her bed, removed her shoes. Kelsey and the other girl were laughing together. A glimpse of Kelsey holding a filmy negligee against her front, cavorting before a mirror. The other girl, opening a closet door. Then, she was alone.

She was awake and yet, strange things were happening in her head. Strange noises, voices, laughter, static. Her husband was knocking at the door which inadvertently she'd locked. She had not meant to lock him out. He was baffled and panicked by the loud music in his house. Yet, she was paralyzed and could not rise from her bed to open the door. *Forgive me! Don't go away, I love you.*

After a while it was quiet downstairs.

In the morning she woke to discover the lights still on downstairs and the rooms ransacked.

Ransacked was the word her husband would use. *Ransacked* was the appropriate word, for the thievery had been random and careless, as children might do.

Missing were silver candlestick holders, silverware and crystal bowls, her husband's laptop from his study. Drawers in her husband's desk had been yanked open, someone had rummaged through his files and papers but carelessly, letting everything fall to the floor.

A small clock, encased in crystal, rimmed in gold, which had been awarded to her husband for one of his history books, and had been kept on the windowsill in front of her husband's desk, was missing.

A rear door was ajar. The house was permeated with cold. In a state of shock Agnes walked through the rooms. She found herself in the same room, repeatedly. As in a troubled dream, she was being made to identify what had been taken from her.

Yet, what the eye does not *see,* the brain can't register.

The effort of remembering was exhausting.

Her head was pounding. Her eyes ached. Her throat was dry and acrid and the inside of her mouth tasted of ashes.

They hadn't ransacked the upstairs. They hadn't found her purse, her wallet and credit cards. They'd respected the privacy of her bedroom . . .

She had no reason to think that her niece had been involved.

Maybe, Kelsey had tried to stop them. But Triste and Mallory had threatened her.

Agnes would never know. She could never ask. She tried to tell herself *It doesn't mean anything—that she doesn't love me. It means only that they were desperate for money.*

Yet she called her sister to ask for Kelsey. Coolly her sister said that Kelsey didn't live with them any longer, Agnes must know this.

Where did Kelsey live? So far as anyone knew, Kelsey lived with "friends."

Kelsey was no longer attending the community college. Agnes must know this.

Bitterly her sister spoke. Though relenting then, realizing it was Agnes, the widowed older sister, to whom she was speaking, and asking why Agnes wanted to speak with Kelsey?

"No reason," Agnes said. "I'm sorry to bother you."

It was terrifying to her, she would probably never see her niece again.

Yet, I still love her.

What was exhausting, when she wasn't "high"—she had to plead for her husband's life.

Hours of each day. And through the night pleading *No! Not ever.*

Not ever give up, I beg you.

As soon as the diagnosis had been made, the doctors had given up on him. So it seemed to the stricken wife.

Repeating their calm rote words *Do you want extraordinary measures taken to sustain your life, in case complications arise during or after surgery* and her husband who was the kindest of men, the most accommodating and least assertive of men, a gentle man, a thoughtful man, a reasonable man, one who would hide his own anxiety and terror in the hope of shielding his wife, had said quietly what the doctor had seemed to be urging him to say *No of course not, doctor. Use your own judgment please.* For this was the brave response. This was the noble response. This was the manly commonsense response. In mounting disbelief and horror Agnes had listened to this exchange and dared to interrupt *No—we're not going to give up. We do want "extraordinary*

measures"—I want "extraordinary measures" for my husband! Please!
Anything you can do, doctor.

She would beg. She would plead. Unlike her beloved husband she could not be stoic in the face of (his) death.

Yet, in the end, fairly quickly there'd been not much the doctors could do. Her husband's life from that hour onward had gone—had departed—swiftly like thread on a bobbin that goes ever more swiftly as it is depleted.

I love you—so many times she told him. Clutching at him with cold frightened fingers.

Love love love you please don't leave me.

She missed him, so much. She could not believe that he would not return to their house. It was that simple.

In the marijuana haze, she'd half-believed—she'd been virtually certain—that her husband was still in the hospital, and wondering why she hadn't come to visit. Or maybe it was in the dream—the dreams—that followed. *High I was so high. The earth was a luminous globe below me and above me—there was nothing . . .*

After he'd died, within hours when she returned to the suddenly cavernous house she'd gone immediately to a medicine cabinet and on the spotless white-marble rim above the sink she had set out pills, capsules—these were sleeping pills, painkillers, antibiotics—that had accumulated over a period of years; prescriptions in both her husband's and her name, long forgotten. *Self-medicating*—yet how much more tempting, to *self-erase*?

There were dozens of pills here. Just a handful, swallowed down with wine or whiskey, and she'd never wake again—perhaps.

"Should I? Should I join you?"—it was ridiculous for the widow to speak aloud in the empty house yet it seemed to her the most natural thing in the world; and what was unnatural was her husband's failure to respond.

She would reason *It's too soon. He doesn't understand what has happened to him yet.*

Weeks now and she hadn't put the pills away. They remained on the marble ledge. Involuntarily her eye counted them—five, eight, twelve, fifteen—twenty-five, thirty-five . . .

She wondered how many sleeping pills, for instance, would be "fatal." She wondered if taking too many pills would produce nausea and vomiting; taking too few, she might remain semi-conscious, or lapse into a vegetative state.

Men were far more successful in suicide attempts than women. This was generally known. For men were not so reluctant to do violence to their bodies: gunshots, hanging, leaping from heights.

I want to die but not to experience it. I want my death to be ambiguous so people will say—It was an accidental overdose!

So people will say—She would not live without him, this is for the best.

What a relief, that Kelsey and her friends hadn't come upstairs to steal from her! They'd respected her privacy, she wanted to think.

How stricken with embarrassment she'd have been if Kelsey had looked into the bathroom and seen the pills so openly displayed. Immediately her niece would have known what this meant, and would have called her mother.

Mom! Aunt Agnes is depressed and suicidal—I thought you should know.

At least, Agnes thought that Kelsey might have made this call.

"Zeke! Thank you."

And, "Zeke—how much do I owe you?"

From a young musician friend, a former student, now years since he'd been an undergraduate student, she'd acquired what she believed to be a higher, purer quality of "pot"—she'd been embarrassed to call him, to make the transaction, pure terror at the possibility—(of course, it was not a likely possibility)—that Zeke was an undercover agent for the local police; she'd encountered him by chance in an organic foods store near the university, he'd been kind to her, asking after her, of course he'd heard that Professor Krauss had died, so very sorry to hear such sad and unexpected news . . . Later she'd called him, set up a meeting at the local mall, in the vast parking lot, she'd been awkward and ashamed and yet determined, laughing so that her face reddened. To Zeke she was Professor Krauss also. To all her admiring students.

A Ziploc bag Zeke sold her. Frankly he'd seemed surprised—then concerned. He'd been polite as she remembered him, from years ago. She told the ponytailed young man she was having friends over for the evening, friends from graduate-student days, Ann Arbor. He'd seemed to believe her. No normal person would much want to *get high* by herself, after all.

As soon as she was safely home she lit a joint and drew in her breath as Kelsey had taught her—cautiously, but deeply. The heat was distracting. She didn't remember such heat. And the dryness, the acridity. Again she began to cough—tears spilled from her eyes. Her husband had said *What are you doing, Agnes? Why are you doing such things? Just come to me, that's all. You know that.*

Mattia.

Running her forefinger down the *Mattia* listings. There were a surprising number—at least a dozen. Most young people had cell phones now. The Mercer County, New Jersey, phone directory had visibly shrunken. Yet, there was a little column of *Mattia*s headed by *Mattia, Angelo.*

His first name hadn't been *Angelo*—she didn't think so.

Maybe—had it been *Eduardo*?

(There was a listing for *Eduardo,* in Trenton.)

Also listed were *Giovanne, Christopher, Anthony, Thomas, E. L. Mattia* . . .

None of these names seemed quite right to her. Yet, she had to suppose that her former student, an inmate-student at Rahway State Prison, was related to one or more of these individuals.

Impulsively she called the listing for *Mattia, Eduardo.*

If there is no answer, then it isn't meant to happen.

The phone rang at the other end. But no one picked up. A recording clicked on—a man's heavily accented voice—quickly Agnes hung up.

Later, she returned to discover the phone directory which she'd left on a kitchen counter, open to the *Mattia* listings. She stared at the column of names. She thought—*Was the name "Joseph"?*

It had been a traditional name, with religious associations. A formal name. When Agnes had addressed the young man it was formally, respectfully—*Mr. Mattia.*

Other instructors in the prison literacy program called students by their first names. But not Agnes, who'd taken seriously the program organizer's warning not to suggest or establish any sort of "inappropriate intimacy" with the inmate-students.

Never touch an inmate. Not even a light tap on the arm.

Never reveal your last name to them. Or where you live, or if you are married.

Agnes remembered with what eagerness she'd read Mattia's prose pieces in her remedial English composition class at Rahway several years before. The teaching experience, for her, in the maximum-security state prison, had been exhausting, but thrilling.

A civic-minded colleague at the university had recruited Agnes who'd been doubtful at first. And Agnes's husband, who thought that prison education was a very good thing, was yet doubtful that Agnes should volunteer. Her training was in Renaissance literature—she'd never taught disadvantaged students of any kind.

She'd told her husband that she would quit the program, if she felt uncomfortable. If it seemed in any way risky, dangerous. But she was determined not to be discouraged and not to drop out. In her vanity, she did not wish to think of herself as *weak, coddled.*

Her university students were almost uniformly excellent, and motivated. For she and her historian-husband taught at a prestigious private university. She'd never taught difficult students, public school students, remedial students or students in any way disabled, or "challenged." At this time she was fifty-three years old and looking much younger, slender, with wavy mahogany-dark hair to her shoulders, and a quick friendly smile to put strangers at ease. She'd done volunteer work mostly for Planned Parenthood and for political campaigns, to help liberal Democrats get elected. She had never visited a prison, even a women's detention facility. She'd learned belatedly that her prison teaching at Rahway was limited to male inmates.

Of her eleven students, eight were African-American; two were "white"; and one was *Mattia, Joseph*—(she was certain now, the name had had an old-world religious association)—who had an olive-dark skin with dark eyes, wiry black hair, an aquiline nose, a small neatly trimmed mustache. Like his larger and more burly fellow inmates Mattia was physically impressive: his shoulders and chest hard-muscled, his neck unusually thick, for one with a relatively slender build. (Clearly, Mattia worked with weights.) Unlike the others he moved gracefully, like an athlete-dancer. He was about five feet eight—inches shorter than the majority of the others.

In the prison classroom Agnes had found herself watching Mattia, in his bright-blue prisoner's coverall, before she'd known his name, struck by his youthful enthusiasm and energy, the *radiance* of his face.

Strange, in a way Mattia was ugly. His features seemed wrong-size for his angular face. His eyes could be stark, staring. Yet, Agnes would come to see him as attractive, even rather beautiful —as others in the classroom sat with dutiful expressions, polite-fixed smiles or faces slack with boredom, Mattia's face seemed to glow with an intense inner warmth.

Agnes had supposed that Mattia was—twenty-five? Twenty-six? The ages of her students ranged from about twenty to forty, so far as she could determine. It would be slightly shocking to Agnes to learn, after the ten-week course ended, that Mattia was thirty-four; that he'd been in Rahway for seven years of a fifteen-year sentence for "involuntary manslaughter"; that he'd enrolled in several courses before hers, but had dropped out before completing them.

The dark-eyed young man had been unfailingly polite to Agnes, whose first name the class had been told, but not her last name. *Ms. Agnes* in Mattia's voice was uttered with an air of reverence as if—so Agnes supposed—the inmate-student saw in her qualities that had belonged to his mother, or to another older woman relative; he was courteous, even deferential, as her university students, who took their professors so much more for granted, were not.

Mattia was the most literate writer in the class, as he was the sharpest-witted, and the most alert. His compositions were childlike, earnest. Yet, his thoughts seemed overlarge for his brain, and writing with a stubby pencil was a means of relieving pressure in the brain; writing in class, as Agnes sat at the front of the room observing, Mattia hunched over his desk frowning and grimacing in a kind of exquisite pain, as if he were talking to himself.

Sometimes, during class discussion, Agnes saw Mattia looking at her—particularly, at *her*—with a brooding expression, in which there was no recognition; at such times, his face was masklike and unsmiling, and seemed rather chilling to her. She hadn't known at the time what his prison sentence was for but she'd thought *He has killed someone. That is the face of a killer.*

But, as if waking from a trance, in the next moment Mattia smiled, and waved his hand for Agnes to call upon him— *Ms. Agnes!*

She loved to hear her name in his velvety voice. She loved to see his eyes light up, and the masklike killer-face vanish in an instant, as if it had never been.

Instructors in the composition course used an expository writing text that was geared for "remedial" readers yet contained essays, in primer English, on such provocative topics as racial integration, women's rights, gay and lesbian rights, freedom of speech and of the press, "patriotism" and "terrorism." There was a section on the history of the American civil rights movement, and there was a section on the history of Native Americans and "European" conquest. Agnes assigned the least difficult of the essays to which her students were to respond in compositions of five hundred words or so. *Just write as if you were speaking to the author. You agree, or disagree—just write down your thought.*

Most of the students were barely literate. In their separate worlds, inaccessible to their instructor, they were likely individuals who aroused fear in others, or at least apprehension; but in the classroom they were disadvantaged as overgrown children. Slowly, with care, Agnes went through their compositions line by line for the benefit of the entire class. The inmate-students had ideas, to a degree—but their ability to express themselves in anything other than simple childish expletives was primitive; and their attitude toward Agnes, respectful at first, if guarded, quickly became sullen and resentful. Even when Agnes tried to praise the "strengths" in their writing, they came to distrust her, for the "suggestions" that were sure to come.

Mattia was quick-witted and shrewd, and usually had no difficulty understanding the essays, but his writing was so strangely condensed, Agnes often didn't know what he was trying to say. It was as if the young man was distrustful of speaking outright. He wrote in the idiom of the street but it was a heightened and abbreviated idiom, succinct as code. From time to time Agnes looked up from one of his tortuous compositions thinking *This is poetry!* When Mattia read his compositions aloud to the class, he read in a way that seemed to convey meaning, yet often the other inmates didn't seem to understand him, either.

She couldn't determine if the other inmates liked Mattia. She couldn't determine if any of the inmates were friends. In the classes, it was common for inmate-students to sit as far apart from one another as they could, including in the farther corners of the room, since, in their cells, as Agnes's supervisor had told her, they were in constant over-close quarters.

When, in class, Agnes questioned Mattia about the meaning of his sentences—(taking care always to be exceedingly considerate and not to appear to be "critical")—Mattia could usually provide the words he'd left out. He seemed not to understand how oblique his meaning was, how baffled the others were.

"We can't read your mind, Joseph"—so Agnes had said.

She'd meant to be playful, and Mattia had looked startled, and then laughed.

"Ms. Agnes ma'am, that is a damn good thing!"

The rest of the inmate-students laughed with Mattia, several of them quite coarsely. Agnes chose to ignore the moment, and to move on.

During the ten-week course, Mattia was the only student not to miss a single class, and Mattia was the only student who handed in every assignment. Though she was to tell no one about him, not her supervisor, not her fellow instructors, and not her husband, Agnes was fascinated by this "Joseph Mattia"—not only his writing ability but also his personality, and his presence. It had always been deeply satisfying to Agnes to teach her university students, but there was no risk involved in teaching them, as the university campus represented no risk to enter; there was no prison protocol to be observed; as an Ivy League professor, she knew that, if she'd never entered her students' lives, their lives would not be altered much, for they'd been surrounded by first-rate teachers for most of their lives. But at Rahway, Ms. Agnes might actually make a difference in an inmate's life, if he allowed it.

Mattia's prose pieces grew more assured with the passage of weeks. He knew, Ms. Agnes thought highly of him: she was one of those adults in authority, one of those members of the *white world,* who held him in high esteem, and would write positively and persuasively on his behalf to the parole board.

I am happy to recommend. Without qualification.

One of my very best students in the course. Gracious, courteous, sense of humor. Trustworthy. Reliable.

It was evident from Mattia's oblique prose pieces that he had committed acts of which he was "ashamed"—but Mattia had not been specific, as none of the inmates were specific about the reasons for which they were in the maximum-security prison. Only after the course had ended did she learn that Mattia had been indicted on a second-degree murder charge, in the death of a Trenton drug dealer; in plea-bargaining negotiations, the charge had been reduced to voluntary manslaughter; finally, to involuntary manslaughter. Instead of twenty years to life for murder, Mattia was serving seven years for manslaughter. Agnes told herself *Probably he was acting in self-defense. Whoever he killed would have killed him. He is not a "killer."*

Mattia's parole had been approved. On the last class day, Mattia had stood before Agnes to thank her.

His lips had trembled. His eyes were awash with tears.

Again she thought *I remind him of—someone. Someone who'd loved him, whom he had loved.*

From his prose pieces, she knew he lived on Tumbrel Street, Trenton, in a neighborhood only a few blocks from the state capital rotunda and the Delaware River. This was a part of Trenton through which visitors to the state capital buildings and the art museum drove without stopping, or avoided altogether by taking Route 29, along the river, into the city. Agnes wondered if he would be returning to this neighborhood; very likely, he had nowhere else to go. How she'd wished, she might invite him to visit *her.*

Or arrange for him to live elsewhere. Away from the environment that had led to his incarceration.

Hesitantly, in a lowered voice so the other inmate-students wouldn't hear as they shuffled out of the classroom, Mattia said, "Ms. Agnes, d'you think I could send you things? Things I would write?"

Agnes was deeply touched. She thought *What is the harm in it? Mattia is not like the others.*

He'd wanted to mail her his "writings," he said. "I never had such a wonderful class, Ms. Agnes. Never learned so much . . ."

Agnes hesitated. She knew, the brave generous reckless gesture would be to give Mattia her address, so that he could write to her; but instructors had been warned against establishing such relations outside the prison classroom; even to allow Mattia to know Agnes's last name was considered dangerous.

"If I knew you would read what I write, I would write more—I would write with *hope*."

Yet still Agnes hesitated.

"I—I'm sorry, Joseph. I guess—that isn't such a good idea."

Mattia smiled quickly. If he was deeply disappointed in her, he spared her knowing.

"Well, ma'am!—thank you. Like I say, I learned *a lot*. Anyway I feel, like—more *hopeful* now."

Agnes was deeply sorry. Deeply disappointed in herself. Such cowardice!

This was a moment, too, when Agnes might have shaken hands with Mattia, in farewell. (She knew that her male instructors violated protocol on such occasions, shaking hands with inmate-students; she'd seen them.) But Agnes was too cautious, and Agnes was aware of guards standing at the doorway, watching her as well as the inmate-students on this last day of class.

"Thank *you*, Joseph! And good luck."

Now, she would make amends.

Several years had passed. If Mattia still lived in Trenton, it would not be such a violation of prison protocol to contact him—would it?

He'd "paid his debt to society"—as it was said. He was a fellow citizen now. She, his former instructor, did not feel superior to him—in her debilitated state, she felt superior to no one—but she did think that, if he still wanted her advice about writing, or any sort of contact with her as a university professor, she might be able to help him.

What had Mattia said, so poignantly—she had given him *hope*.

And from him, perhaps she would acquire *hope*.

She was getting high more frequently. Alone in the cavernous house.

It was good for her, she thought. Saved her life!—for she'd had no appetite since her husband's death, in fact since his hospitalization when food—the "eating" of "food"—came to seem nauseating to her as well as bizarre.

Placing "food" in a mouth, "eating"—it had become mechanical to her, a learned act and not a natural instinct. (She'd lost so much weight, her clothing hung over her as on a scarecrow. But why should she care? There was no one to *see*.)

But now, since she'd begun smoking, her appetite had returned—a ferocious appetite, as of a young child, requiring nourishment in order to grow. She devoured yogurt by the quart container, mixed with blueberries and raspberries (her husband's favorite fruits), and sometimes in the semi-darkened bedroom listening to rain pelting the roof close above her head she devoured containers of crackers—"gourmet" crackers—dipped into hummus and smeared with soft, stale cheese. It was far too much trouble for her to "prepare" any meal—she could not bear the ritual of such preparation, in the empty kitchen.

Yet it was a good thing, she was eating now. At least, sporadically and hungrily. Smiling to think *I will not starve to death, at least!*

A few months after she'd begun, smoking "pot" was becoming as ritualized to her as having a glass of wine had been for her husband, before every meal. She had sometimes joined him, but usually not—wine made her sleepy, and in the night it gave her a headache, or left her feeling, in the morning, mildly depressed. She knew that alcohol was a depressant to the nervous system and that she must avoid it, like the pills on the marble ledge.

Getting high was a different sensation. *Staying high* was the challenge.

Mattia might be a source of marijuana, too. She hadn't thought of this initially but—yes: probably.

(He'd been incarcerated for killing a drug dealer. It wasn't implausible to assume that he might have dealt in drugs himself.)

(Or, he might have cut himself out from his old life entirely. He might be living now somewhere else.)

(She wasn't sure which she hoped for—only that she wanted very much to see him again, and to make amends for her cowardice.)

Getting high gave her clarity: she planned how she would seek out Joseph Mattia. Shutting her eyes she rehearsed driving to Trenton, fifteen miles from the village of Quaker Heights; exiting at the State Capitol exit, locating Tumbrel Street . . . None of the Mattias listed in the directory lived on Tumbrel Street in Trenton but Eduardo Mattia lived on Depot Avenue which was close by Tumbrel—(so Agnes had determined from a city map)—and there was Anthony Mattia on Seventh Street and

E. L. Mattia—(a woman?)—on West State Street, also close by. A large family—the Mattias.

In this neighborhood, she could make inquiries about "Joseph Mattia"—if she dared, she could go to one of the Mattia addresses, and introduce herself.

Do you know Joseph Mattia? Is he a relative of yours?
Joseph is a former student of mine who'd been very promising.
Hello! My name is—
Hello! I am a former teacher of Joseph Mattia.
Her heart began pounding quickly, in this fantasy.
Getting high was a dream. *Waking* was the fear.

In the cavernous house the phone rang frequently. She pressed her hands over her ears.

"Nobody's home! Leave me alone."

She had no obligation to pick up a ringing phone. She had no obligation to return email messages marked CONCERNED—or even to read them.

Since getting high she was avoiding relatives, friends. They were dull "straight" people—*getting high* to them meant alcohol, if anything.

Of course they would disapprove of her behavior. Her husband would disapprove. She could not bear them talking about her.

Sometimes, the doorbell rang. Upstairs she went to see who it might be, noting the car in the driveway.

Her sister called, left a message. Upsetting news about—who was it—the daughter—the niece, Kelsey—an arrest—or, had

Kelsey fled arrest?—Agnes deleted the message without hearing the end.

(Only vaguely could Agnes remember the young people who'd invaded her house—Kelsey's friends Triste?—Randi?—the other, who'd looked at Agnes with the cold bemused eyes of a killer, she'd refused to acknowledge. If he went on to kill another hapless, foolish victim, what was that to *her*?)

Those visitors, importunate and "concerned"—she knew she must deflect them, to prevent them calling 911. She would make a telephone call and hurriedly leave a message saying that she was fine but wanted to be alone for a while; or, she would send a flurry of emails saying the same thing.

Alone alone alone she wanted alone. Except for Joseph Mattia.

Another time making a purchase from her musician-friend Zeke. And another time. And each time, the price was escalating.

The third time, Agnes asked Zeke about this: the price of a Ziploc bag of "joints." And with a shrug Zeke said, "It's the market, Agnes. Supply and demand."

The reply was indifferent, even rude. Zeke did not seem to care about *her.*

She was hurt. She was offended. Didn't he respect Professor Krauss any longer? The way *Agnes* had rolled off his tongue, and not *Professor Krauss.*

She would find someone else to supply her! Nonetheless, on this occasion, she paid.

* * *

Her first drive to Tumbrel Street, Trenton. Five months, three weeks and two days after the call had come from the hospital summoning her, belatedly.

Getting high gave her the courage. Strength flowing through her veins!

In her expansive floating mood she knew to drive slowly—carefully. She smiled to think how embarrassing it would be, to be arrested by police for a D.U.I.—at her age.

In the car she laughed aloud, thinking of this.

The car radio was tuned now to the Trenton AM station. Blasting rap music, rock, high-decibel advertisements. *Fat Joe. Young Jeezy. Ne-Yo. Tyga. Cash Out.* She understood how such sound assailing her ears was an infusion of strength, courage.

Such deafening sound, and little room for fear, caution. Little room for *thought.*

It was *thought* that was the enemy, Agnes understood. Getting high meant rising above *thought.*

She exited Route 1 for the state capital buildings. Through a circuitous route involving a number of one-way streets and streets barricaded for no evident reason she made her way to Tumbrel Street which was only two blocks from State Street and from the Delaware River. This was a neighborhood of decaying row houses and brownstones—boarded-up and abandoned stores. It was tricky—treacherous!—to drive here for the narrow streets were made narrower by parked vehicles.

Very few "white" faces here. Agnes was feeling washed-out, anemic.

It was a neighborhood of very dark-skinned African-Americans and others who were light-skinned, possibly African-American and/or Hispanic. Eagerly she looked for *him*.

Turning onto Seventh Street and State Street which was a major thoroughfare in Trenton she saw more "white" faces—and many pedestrians, waiting for buses.

Why did race matter so much? The color of *skin*.

She could love anyone, Agnes thought. Skin-color did not mean anything to her, only the soul within.

Mattia's liquid-dark eyes. Fixed upon her.

Ms. Agnes I feel like—more hopeful now.

A half hour, forty minutes Agnes drove slowly along the streets of downtown Trenton. Tumbrel to West State Street and West State Street to Portage; Portage to Hammond, and Grinnell Park; right turn, and back to Tumbrel which was, for a number of blocks, a commercial street of small stores—Korean food market, beauty salon, nail salon, wig shop, diner, tavern. And a number of boarded-up, graffiti-marked stores. Trenton was not an easy city to navigate since most of the streets were one-way. And some were barricaded—under repair. (Except there appeared to be no workers repairing the streets, only just abandoned-looking heavy equipment.) She saw men on the street who might have been Joseph Mattia yet were not. Yet, she felt that she was drawing closer to him.

She told herself *I have nothing else to do. This is my only hope.*

Her husband would be dismayed! She could hardly bring herself to think of him, how he would feel about her behavior now; how concerned he would be. He'd promised to "protect" her—as a young husband he'd promised many things—but of course he had not been able to protect her from his own mortality. She'd been a girl when he'd met her, at the University of Michigan. Her hair dark brown, glossy-brown, and her eyes bright and alert. Now, her hair had turned silver. It was really a remarkable hue, she had only to park her car, to walk along the sidewalk—here, on Tumbrel Street—to draw eyes to her, startled and admiring.

Ma'am you are beautiful!

Whatever age you are ma'am—you lookin good.

Ma'am—you someone I know, is you?

These were women mostly. Smiling black women.

For this walk in Trenton she wore her good clothes. A widow's tasteful clothes, black cashmere. And the cloche hat on her silvery hair. And good shoes—expensive Italian shoes she'd purchased in Rome, the previous summer traveling with her historian-husband.

They'd also gone to Florence, Venice, Milano, Delphi. Her husband had brought along one of his numberless guidebooks— this one titled *Mysteries of Delphi*. She'd been astonished to see, superimposed upon photographs of the great ruined sites, color transparencies indicating the richness of color of the original sites—primary colors of red and blue—and extraordinary ornamental detail that suggested human specificity instead of "classic" simplicity. Of course, Agnes should have known, but had never thought until her husband explained to her, that the ancient temples weren't classics of austerity—pearl-colored, luminous, stark—but vari-colored, even garish. Ruins had not always been *ruins*. Like most tourists she'd assumed that the ancient sites had always been, in essence, what they were at the present time. Like most tourists she hadn't given much thought to what she was seeing and her thoughts were naïve and uninformed. Her husband had said *The way people actually live is known only to them. They take their daily lives with them, they leave just remnants for historians to decode.*

He had opened that world of the past to her. And now, he himself had become *past*.

She thought *He took everything with him. No one will remember who he was—or who I was.*

She was beginning to feel very strange. A lowering of blood pressure—she knew the sensation. Several times during the hospital vigil and after his death she'd come close to fainting, and twice she had found herself on the floor, dazed and uncomprehending. The sensation began with a darkening of vision, as color bleached out of the world; there came then a roaring in her ears, a feeling of utter sorrow, lostness, futility . . .

At the intersection of Seventh Street and Hammond, out of a corner bodega he stepped carrying a six-pack of beer.

He was older of course. He must have been—nearly forty.

His dark hair threaded with gray was longer than she recalled, his eyes were deep-socketed and red-lidded. His skin seemed darker, as if smudged. And he was wearing civilian clothes, not the bright-blue prison coverall that had given to the most hulking inmates a look of clownishness—his clothes were cheaply stylish, a cranberry-colored shirt in a satiny fabric, open at the throat; baggy cargo pants, with deep pockets and a brass-buckle belt riding low on his narrow hips.

She saw, in that instant: the narrowed eyes, the aquiline nose, the small trim mustache on the upper lip. And something new— through his left eyebrow, a wicked little zipperlike scar.

It was Joseph Mattia!—(was it?). Recognizing her, but having forgotten her name.

He'd stopped dead in his tracks. As a predator, sighting prey, though he has not been hunting and is not even hungry, will stop dead in his tracks by instinct, staring. And then very slowly he smiled as an indecipherable light came up in his eyes.

"Ma'am! You lookin *good*."

Toad-Baby

Out of the corner of her silverfish eye Momma is watching me to see if I am sleeping. *I am not sleeping I am wide awake.*

Came to stay with Momma. Though I don't live here now.

I was eleven first time I ran away. Stayed with my friend Sadie but didn't tell them why, or not exactly. Could not tell anyone exactly for they use your words against you like rubbing a dirty rag in your face saying it is your own dirtiness, you deserve it.

Cop brought me back that time. Momma and Evander hid how mad they were that I'd shamed them, beat me real bad after the cop left.

Evander is gone now. Left his little son behind Momma says like you'd leave an ugly nigger-toad behind.

Momma's family is disgusted with her for having this new baby who cries all the time. Bulgy toad-eyes, and skin kind of toad-colored, and a drooly little mouth, and floppy arms and legs like there's no bone inside.

Momma grabbed and hugged me this time I came in. Hid her hot face in my neck till I pushed her away smelling her breath.

It is not normal for a grown woman to hide her face against her thirteen-year-old daughter and cry in such a way.

Her and me the same height now but Momma is forty pounds heavier, and her skin scalding-hot.

I am placed in a "foster home" by the county but it is with my aunt who is Momma's oldest sister, half-sister as my aunt Chloe and Momma had different fathers.

At school the teacher asks me to help with the math lesson. At the blackboard I was wearing a red-patterned scarf tied at the neck, that was my aunt Chloe's scarf. Another time, my brass-colored hair was plaited in cornrows, that aunt Chloe had done. I am a big girl for thirteen. And I stand tall. I don't take shit from even the big boys, just look them eye-to-eye. I'm the one that knows the answer to the math problems not them.

Who is that girl, another teacher in the hall said looking into the room, she'd mistaken me for a teacher's aide from the college. I just laughed and did not speak fast or excited but calm as I have learned and clear-eyed meeting their eyes.

A blush came into my face, they were looking so hard at me.

But I never tell them anything of Momma, or of Toad-Baby who is my young brother. Even when they ask, and touch my wrist to show they are sincere and want to help, if there is help needed by me, I never say anything that is real but only just *Things are OK at home. Things are good.*

Then I laugh, to show that I am all right. If they touch my wrist I throw off the touch without seeming-so.

Who it was who'd beat my father to death, I don't know. Momma told police she did not see any faces and did not hear any voices and when she came out of hiding, it was all over.

I was three years old then. I don't remember any of that time or even where it was but I know that it was somewhere else, not where Momma lives now.

It is like a wall that has been hosed down, that time. What was there is faded and torn and even if you touch it with your fingers to help you read what it was, you can't.

Momma did not mean to hurt Toad-Baby but Momma is very sad and tired sometimes. And Momma's breath smells sour, those bad times.

Sometimes, Momma is angry. *Why is this my life? This is not my life.*

Momma says *That minute he stuck it in me, if I could remove that. Then I wouldn't have this ugly nigger-toad-baby. I would not be here in this place undersea.* Momma looks at me with her eyes glinting like silverfish and the eyelids scraped raw.

It's scary when Momma speaks like this. I wish she would not.

Momma says *A baby is too big to fit inside a woman. Better to have eggs that hatch like birds or snakes, you wouldn't even have to be there.*

When Evander went away Momma'd had accidents with Toad-Baby dropping him on the stairs where she was stumbling, and the lightbulb burnt out. Bad bruises on Toad-Baby's head and a "concussion" they said at the ER where they asked me questions as Momma had needed me to come along with her and I told them that my baby brother squirmed and kicked and got loose of Momma's arms and fell and maybe they believed me, or maybe not.

Seeing Toad-Baby with his dark, dense hair and mottled skin, they could see he was a *mix-race baby*. If they held this against Momma they did not show it like Momma's family did.

Momma is *self-medicated* she calls it. Keeping her thoughts from turning bad, she says. Like backed-up drains, the way your own thoughts can strangle you in your sleep.

Last night here at Momma's. She'd looked at me strange like wanting to scream at me *Why are you here, I don't need you!* Helped Momma with supper and cleanup in the kitchen. And putting Toad-Baby to bed. Trying then to stay awake watching late-night TV. And Toad-Baby fussing and kicking in his crib. And Momma sees that my eyes are shutting and takes advantage getting up from the sofa soft-barefoot-walking into the bathroom to fill the tub and bring Toad-Baby inside to bathe with her because she does not want to be alone. I can't let Momma shut the door, I will have to bang on the door and break it down if I can, and then Momma's nightgown is wet and Toad-Baby's diaper is soaked and has to be changed. My hands are shaking, I promised Momma I would protect him for there is no one else.

I am Toad-Baby's only sister. I am eleven years older than Toad-Baby and I think that he will never know me really, I will always be his old sister. And my skin-color different from his. These days will be long forgotten for his skin-color will draw him away from us to live with his own kind and not us, Momma says.

You won't let it happen, will you?—Momma is begging me.

For Momma does not want to hurt Toad-Baby.

We are lying on Momma's bed, and baby is between us. Again I am afraid of sleeping though I am very tired.

Momma has been drinking, so Momma is happy. But Momma's mood can change, when she is happy. Momma says I can drown only one of you so which one will it be?

Damn, Momma! That is not funny.

Momma laughs and shudders. Only thing 'bout me that's funny is my face.

But truly, Momma does not want to hurt Toad-Baby.

Except, Toad-Baby cries so loud. You would not think such a tiny baby can cry so loud, your thoughts are rattled like dried peas shaken inside a cup. And then Momma becomes excitable, and anxious.

I stayed awake those times. Pinched my cheek, bit the inside of my mouth till it bled.

You can't keep your eyelids from closing. No more than you can keep the dark from lifting from the earth.

Momma, stop! Struggling grunting with Momma to pull the baby out of the tub. The water is at the top, and steaming. Spilling over onto the floor. Momma slaps me so I am knocked down onto the slippery floor trying to get my balance and there is Toad-Baby on the floor and not crying, or kicking. All wet and streaming water Toad-Baby is so little-looking like a floppy doll quiet and not squirming, kicking or shrieking and Momma snatches him up and shakes him and still, Toad-Baby does not cry. And I take Toad-Baby from Momma shouting into Momma's face, grab Toad-Baby out of Momma's hands and squeeze his little chest not knowing what I am doing in my desperation laying Toad-Baby back onto the puddled floor and onto his back pressing my mouth against the little snail mouth and breathing, and breathing, and breathing hard and deep inside into the mouth until at last Toad-Baby begins to stir, and fret, and cry. Toad-Baby sucks in air, you can hear. Toad-Baby's bellowing cries, that Momma has said pierced her heart but Momma is crying now, too. On her knees on the bathroom floor. Momma's wet hair in her face and it's a surprise I see that Momma is a girl too—a girl like me but older, and her skin hot like sunburn. And she hugs me and starts to cry, God will bless you, you have protected your baby brother from the wrath of God.

And so after this, all my life I will be fearful of sleeping. It is a terrible temptation to close your eyes, and sleep. But Toad-Baby's cries will wake me, long after Toad-Baby is gone into his own life. Long after Momma is gone and I will be an old woman, Toad-Baby's cries will wake me out of the dark.

Demon

Demon-child. Kicked in the womb so his poor young mother doubled over in pain. Nursing he tugged and tore at her breasts. Wailed through the night. Puked, shat. Refused to eat. *No I am loving, I am mad with love.* Of Mama. (Though fearful of Da.) Curling burrowing pushing his head into Mama's arms, against Mama's warm fleshy body. Starving for love, food. Starving for what he could not know yet to name: *God's grace, salvation.*

Sign of Satan: flamey-red ugly-pimply birthmark snake-shaped. On his underjaw, coiled below his ear. Almost you can't see it. A little boy he's teased by neighbor girls, hulking big girls with titties and laughing-wet eyes. *Demon! Demon! Look it, the sign of the Demon!*

Those years. Passing in a fever-dream. Or maybe never passed. Mama prayed over him, hugged and slapped. He was her baby, her Jethro. She had named him, as she had borne him. But now she could not love him. Shook him. In the wink of an eye, Mama was not young. Shook his skinny shoulders so his head rocked. Minister prayed over him. *Deliver us from evil* and he was good, he *was* delivered from evil. Except at the school his eyes misted over, couldn't see the blackboard. White chalk in the teacher's fingers striking the board hurt his ears, sharp clicking sound so he winced and wetted his pants.

Nasty and stupid the teacher called him. Not like the other children.

If not *like the other children,* then like *who? What?*

Those years. How many years. As in a stalled city bus, diesel exhaust pouring out the rear. Stink of it everywhere. Da had gone away and left them, Mama sat at the kitchen table fat-thighed and her knees raddled. Same view through same flyspecked windows. Year after year the battered-tin diner, vacant lot swooning with weeds and rubble glitter of broken glass and the path worn through it slantwise where children ran shouting above the river. Broken pavement littered like confetti from a parade long past.

Or maybe it was the pledge of something vast, infinite. You could never come to the end of it. Wavering and blinding in blasts of light. *Desert* maybe. *Red desert* where demons dance, swirl in the hot winds. Never seen an actual *desert* except pictures, a name on a map. And in his head swelling to burst.

Demon-child they whispered of him. But no, he was loving, mad with love. Too small, too short. Stunted legs. Head too big for his spindly shoulders. Strange waxy-pale moon-face, almond eyes beautiful if you took care to look, small wet mouth perpetually sucking inward. As if to keep the bad words, words of filth and damnation, safely inside.

The sign of Satan coiled on his underjaw began to fade. Like the skin eruptions of adolescence. Blood drawn gradually back into tissue, capillaries.

Not a demon-child after all but a shy anxious loving child with the Bible-name no one could pronounce—*Jeth-ro*. Betrayed by the eyes of others seeking always to laugh and to sneer. Betrayed by having been squeezed from the womb before he was ready.

Not a demon-child but for years he rode wild thunderous razor-hooved black stallions by night and by day. Furious galloping on sidewalks, in asphalt playgrounds where his classmates lay fallen, bleeding and dying. The older boys who tormented him, the older girls giggling and poking him through his pants—*Jeth'o! Jeth!* Through the school corridors trampling all in his way including teachers, adults. Among them the innocent children, casualties of war. Furious tearing hooves, froth-flecked nostrils, bared teeth, God's wrath, the black stallion rearing, whinnying. *I destroy all in my path. I was born without mercy.*

Not a demon-child but he torched the school where they'd laughed at him, rows of stores, run-down wood frame houses in the neighborhood with rotting stoops to the sidewalk like his own. Many times the smelly bed where Mama and Da had hidden from him, when he'd been a baby. And no one knew of the raging flames, and continued as before in ignorance of the demon among them *born without mercy.*

This January morning bright and windy and he's staring at a face floating in a mirror. Dirty mirror in a public lavatory at the Trailways bus station. The man's face appears beside his, looming above his like a moon. The face larger, stained teeth glistening in a wet sly smile. Maybe at one of the churches, he'd seen this face. Maybe it was Mama who'd introduced them. One of the ministers, to take the place of the elder. And the fingers clutching at his, that little (secret) tickle of the thumb against the palm of his hand, so he'd laughed, and shivered, and was ashamed. And now, that face has followed him here. In the mirror beside his. And the hands touching him, tickling at first, and then harder so he could not break away and he could not breathe for something tarry-black flew up to his face, covering his mouth, his mouth and his nose, he could not breathe and began to fall into the tarry blackness, and the hands gripped him, and the arms gripped him, and the mouth sucked at him, and he opened his mouth to scream but could not. And a door opened and there came a shout *Hey! What are you perverts doing! Jesus.* And the voice faded, the door was shut again in revulsion. The man-who-was-a-minister was gone. He wasn't sure, he'd thought it was a minister, and Mama had thought he was, but Mama was sometimes mistaken and when this was so, Mama would not admit her mistake and became very excited if you tried to correct her. The side of his head hurt, he opened his eyes not knowing at first where he was then seeing he was lying on a filthy floor partway inside a toilet stall. And urinals along the wall, filthy. And sink and mirror splotched with filth. And the smells, he could not breathe. Where he'd been dropped, like garbage. Dropped and kicked in the chest, with the hope that his heart would cease beating but it had not. To his shame he saw that his trousers had been opened, the front of his trousers crudely unzipped and the zipper broken and Mama would know, if the zipper was broken. He was breathing now but so shallowly he could not catch his breath. He was crying, and he was whimpering. Someone came to lift him by the underarms, in disgust. *Get out of here. Go away from here. Shame! The age you are! Never come back here, go away to Hell where you belong.* Barely he could walk, the pain between his legs was so severe. Pain in the crack of his ass, the tender skin broken, bleeding. Barely could he make his way through the bus station waiting room where every eye was fixed upon him in revulsion and mirth.

Demon-child. Look!

Crawling away to die. Where he'd hidden. One of the boarded-up buildings on the river. Crawl through a window, and inside. Dropping to the cellar floor. And there, a metallic surface in which the face awaited except now he saw how the mark of Satan was upon him, in his right eyeball a speck of dirt? dust? blood? Where at last the demon has been released. For it is the New Year. Shifting of Earth's axis. For to be away from what is familiar, like walking on a sharp-slanted floor, allows *something other* in. Or the *something other* has been inside you all along and until now you do not realize.

With a strange sick calm he knows. Knows even before he has seen: sign of Satan. In the yellowish-white of his eyeball. Not the coiled little snake but the five-sided star: *pentagram.*

The ministers had warned. Five-sided star: *pentagram.*

It is there, in his right eye. He rubs at it frantically with his fist.

Runs home, two miles. He's a familiar sight here though no one knows his name. Mama knows there's been trouble, has he lied about taking his medication? Hiding the capsule under his tongue then spitting it out? Jesus yes but you can't oversee every minute with one like him. Yes he was born wrong and nobody's fault, nobody'd told any of us don't smoke don't drink that shit they tell the young mothers today nobody told us, like nobody told our mothers or their mothers, see? Yes but God must've wanted it this way. Yes but your love wears out like the lead backing of a cheap mirror corroding the glass. Yes but you have prayed and prayed and cursed the words not echoing up to God but downward into an empty smelly well.

Nineteen years old, and stunted-growth like a dwarf, or almost. And the rounded shoulders of a dwarf. Shaved-head glinting blue. Little bumps, knobs and shallows in the shaved-head, and a constellation of pale freckles. People thought he'd been sick, his hair had fallen out, he was so skinny, gangly-limbed. But luminous shining eyes women at church knew to be beautiful. And on the street, where he'd wandered miles. Strangers, smiling at him. Smiling nervously, tensely at him. Smiling as Christians are bade to do, not to judge. And in the neighborhood near his home he was known by a first name like a Bible name—*Jethro*. Weird sweet boy but excitable, couldn't look you in the eye. Twitching his shoulders like in a spasm like he's shrugging out of somebody's grip.

Fast as you can run, somebody else runs faster!

Or, pursuing you in a vehicle. Horn honking, and guys screaming out the window. *Freaky Jethro. Sick perv. Fag.*

In the place they are living now, row house on Mill Street he's pressing his knuckly hands against his ears not hearing his drunk Mama shouting why is he home so early, has a job in a lumber yard five-minute walk away so why isn't he there? Pushes past the drunk fat woman and into the bathroom, shuts the door and there in the mirror Oh God it has returned: five-sided star, *pentagram*. Unmistakable sign of Satan. Embedded deep in the right eyeball below the dilated pupil.

No! No! God help.

Goes wild, rubs with both fists, pokes with fingers. He's sobbing, praying. Beats at himself, fists and nails. His sister now pounding on the door what is it? What's wrong? Jeth? And Mama's voice loud and frightened. It *has happened,* he thinks. First clear thought *Has happened, now everyone will see.* Like a stone sinking in water, so clear and so calm. Because he has always known the prayers were useless. On your knees bowing your head inviting Jesus into your heart but why should Jesus come into *your heart* that's so freaky-ugly, and the heart of a fag? Sign of the demon would return, absorbed into his blood but must one day re-emerge.

Pushes past the women and in the kitchen paws through drawers scattering cutlery that falls to the floor, there's the long carving knife, his fingers shut about it like fate. Again pushes past the women without taking notice of them, shoves aside his heavyset sister as lightly as he lifts lumber, armloads of bricks. Hasn't he prayed to Our Father to be perfect as a machine, many times? A machine does not think, and a machine does not feel. A machine does not starve for love. A machine *does.*

Inside the bathroom and the door shut and locked behind him against the screaming women. Whispering to the frightened face in the mirror *Away Satan! Away Satan! Jesus help me.* Steadying his right wrist with the fingers of his left hand, in the fingers of his right hand gripping the carving knife, bringing it to the eyeball, unable to resist wincing, blinking, jerking away with a whimper—but again forcing himself to bring the tip of the knife to the eyeball, and with a boldness borne of desperation inserting and twisting the accursed eyeball. *Yes! Now! It is in.* Pain so colossal it could not be measured—like the sky. Burning cleansing roaring sensation as of utter surprise, astonishment. A blast of fire. The eyeball is not easy to dislodge, it is connected by sinewy tissue to the interior of the socket, he must pull at it with his bloody fingers, moaning, not knowing that it is he who is moaning, sawing with the sharper edge of the knife. Manages to cut the eyeball free, like Mama squeezing baby out of her belly into this pig trough of sin and filth and defilement, no turning back until Jesus calls you home.

He drops the eyeball into the stained toilet, flushes the toilet with shaky slippery-excited fingers. And the sign of the demon is *gone.*

One eye socket empty and fresh-bleeding like tears and he is on his knees praying Thank you God! Thank you Jesus! weeping with joy as angels in radiant garments with eyes of blinding brightness reach down to embrace him not mindful of his red-slippery mask of a face and not mindful that he is freaky, a perv or a fag, for he is none of these now, now he is himself an angel of God, now he will float into the sky above the Earth where, some wind-blustery January morning you will see him, or a face like his, in a furious cloud.

Lorelei

Please love me my eyes beg. My need is so raw, I can't blame any
of you from looking quickly away.

Not you, not you, and you—none of you can I blame. *Only
just love me, can't you? Love me . . .*

That Sunday night, desperate not to be late, I had to change
trains at Times Square, and the subway was jammed, both trains
crowded, always I knew it would happen soon, my destiny would
happen within the hour, except: it was required that I be at the
precise position when you lift your eyes to mine (casual-seeming,
by chance) as you turn to face me. I must be there, or the precious moment will pass, and then—so lonely! In the swarm of
strangers departing a train, pushing into the next train, pushing
to the gritty stairs, breathless and trying not to turn my ankle
in my spike-heeled sandals, my hair so glossy black you'd sus-
pect it must be dyed but *my hair is not dyed, this is my natural
hair-color*, and my skin white, exquisite soft-skinned white, and
I'm wearing a black suede short skirt to mid-thigh and black

diamond-patterned stockings with a black satin garter belt you can catch a glimpse of when I'm seated and I cross my slender legs in just the right, practiced way; and a white lace camisole, and beneath the camisole a black satin lace bra that grips my small breasts tight lifting them in mute appeal. *Please love me, please look at me, how can you look away? Here I am, before you.* My shiny-black hair I have ratted with a steel comb to three times its natural size, my mouth that's small and hurt like a snail in its shell I have outlined in crimson, a high-gloss lipstick applied to the outside of the lips enlarging them so I'm breathless smiling making my way to the far side of the track being pushed-against, collided-with, rudely touched by—who?—sometimes I feel one of you brush against me light as a feather's touch, purely by accident, or almost-accident, sometimes it's a hurtful jolt, I could step aside if I'm alert enough but a strange lassitude overcomes me, this one isn't the one, and yet!—the shock of him colliding with me as he hurries past, scarcely aware of me, doesn't slow his pace or apologize, not even a murmured *Excuse me,* the touch is like an electric shock, half-pleasurable, though meant to hurt. As if he knows, this stranger, that he isn't the one. Not tonight.

That Sunday night, not late—not yet 10 P.M. And not so crowded as the previous nights, those wild weekend nights, but still plenty crowded at Times Square, you can be sure. And I was the desperate girl you saw hurrying to make the downtown train. Before the doors closed. Stumbling in my high-heeled shoes so you might have thought there was something wrong with me, the over-bright glisten in my black-mascara eyes and parted crimson lips, the look in my feverish face of anticipation and dread, you'd have felt a stab of pity, and maybe something else, something deeper than pity, and more cruel, and possibly you'd offered to help me, offered your seat to me at least. And possibly, I'd have accepted.

Always in the subway I think *On this train, this train is my destiny: who? Which one of you?* Tremulous with excitement. Anticipation. Pondering through my lowered eyelashes the possibilities. Mostly men of course but (sometimes) women also. Young men, middle-aged men, occasionally older men. Young women, with a certain sign. But never middle-aged, or older women. Never. I tried not even to look at them. Resented them, their raddled faces and tired eyes. And sometimes in those eyes a look of hope, which I particularly despised. For in the hopeless, hope is obscene! And when out of sheer loneliness one of these women smiles at me, moves over inviting me to sit beside her, like hell I will sit next to some old bag like she's my mother, or grandmother!

As if I would ever be one of *them*.

On the train that night a woman of about forty-five took shrewd note of me as soon as I entered the car, out of breath and laughing to myself, my hair just slightly disheveled, fallen into my face. The woman was wearing a green uniform, and ugly dirty-white nurse's shoes they looked like, and her dirt-colored hair flat against her head in a hairnet, staring at me not with sympathy or pity but with disapproval I thought, prissy fish-mouth I tried not to look at. Hate that type of person observing me, judging me coolly. Not to the hairnet woman was I pleading *Look at me, love me! Hey: here I am.*

In the subway the trains move so swiftly you can never catch your breath. Outside the grimy window that's a reflecting surface like a mirror mostly there are the rushing tunnel walls, that slow as the train slows for a station, and the doors open with a pneumatic hiss like the sigh of a great ugly beast, and passengers lurch off, and new passengers lurch on, and I lift my eyes hopeful and yearning *Who will be my destiny? Which one of you?* At Thirty-fourth Street one of you entered the car, sat near me, I could see that he'd chosen the seat beside me deliberately, for there were other, unoccupied seats. The way his eyes trailed over me like slow slugs, my crossed legs in the patterned black stockings, my mouth in a dreamy half-smile, as if I'm expecting to recognize a friend. A friendly face. Like a child hoping to be pleasantly surprised, for I am not a cynical person by nature. And he stared at me appraising. His mouth moved into a kind of smile. He was many years older than I was, one of the bad-Daddys of the subway. In the underground are the bad-Daddys, you know one another. Staring rudely, with that smile at the edge of a sneer, or a sneer at the edge of a smile. In his early forties, pale coarse pitted skin attractive in that battered way some men are, that would be hopeless laughable ugliness in a female. Sand-colored hair crimped and wavy like a wig, and in his right earlobe a silver ear cuff looking as if it might hurt, like something clamped into the flesh. *The sign* that took my eye immediately was that he was wearing suede, which matched my skirt: a black jacket with chrome studs. (The jacket was not "real" suede of course. My skirt, that strained at my thighs just inches below the fork in my legs, was not "real" suede of course.) He was wearing dark trousers and (fake) ostrich-skin boots. On his (hairy) left wrist, a heavy ID bracelet. When he opened his mouth to smile, there was the shock of a gleaming tongue-ring winking at me. As if he knew me he spoke a name, had to be a name he'd invented at that moment, or maybe it was a name known to him, of a girl he'd known and had not seen in years, and I smiled at him saying no that is not my name, I am not that girl, and he asked *Which girl are you, then?* And the tongue-ring winked at me in a nasty way, unmistakable. And I told him *Lorelei—I am Lorelei.* And he cupped his hand to his ear as if hard-of-hearing in the noisy subway train and he repeated the name *Lorelei* and added *A beautiful name for a beautiful girl.* It was not clear to me if he spoke these words truly or in jest but I saw that he was excited by me. I saw the light come into his eyes, that were ordinary small mud-colored eyes. In a lowered voice he began speaking of himself, said he was a lonely pilgrim searching for something he could not name, been searching for all of his life, would I like to have a drink with him, please would I like to have a drink with him, we could get off at the next stop and have a drink together, he knew just the place, and all this time I was quietly observing him, through my mascara-lashes I was observing him, his eyes that were ordinary and mud-colored and hopeful and the truth came to me *No: he is not the one.* So politely I told him I could not get off the train with him, no thank you. Told him that I was meeting someone else. And he stared at me not-so-friendly now, and spoke to me in a low crude voice not-so-friendly now, exposing the spit-gleaming tongue-ring not-so-friendly now, called me *Lorelei* like it was *Loora-Lee* and some kind of stupid name, cow-name, he didn't think so much of. All this while other passengers in the train were trying not to observe us, trying not to hear the man speaking to me, the way you'd speak to (maybe) a retarded girl in the train, a girl her family ought not to have let ride the train alone, that kind of girl, but I am not that girl of course. One of those eavesdropping was the hairnet woman in the ugly green uniform, I saw now was food-stained, had to be a cafeteria worker probably, so I could pity *her*. The hairnet woman was frowning at both of us like we were the scum of the earth, so I could despise *her*.

Shutting my eyes then, and not opening them until later, several stops later, the hairnet woman was gone and the tongue-ring man in the seat beside me was gone and I checked my reflection in my little gold mirror compact seeing a shiny nose, anxious eyes for I had almost made a mistake. *That one was a test. In your ignorance you might have gone with him.*

For my life at that time was a continual testing. That in ignorance or desperation I would make a terrible error, and would not realize my destiny.

Slamming into the car from the car ahead was a big girl of about thirty with no eyelashes like she'd plucked them all out or shaved them, and she'd shaved most of her head so just stiff platinum-blond quills remained, so striking!—everybody in the car stared at her even those who'd been nodding off woke to take in such a sight. The girl's face was glowing and shiny as if made of some synthetic material like flesh-plastic, with no pores, and her lips were swollen and pouty, and moved as if she was talking to herself. For in the subway, some of us sometimes talk to ourselves, and you are (maybe) meant to overhear. Seeing me, her eyes latching onto mine, she stopped in mid-stride and stood swaying above me holding the rail about two feet from me, observing me and a slow smile broke over the plastic-face like something melting. Big husky girl six feet tall in khakis and tight-fitting black T-shirt with DRAGO FREK in red letters. *The sign* was a bullet-shape silver ring on the middle finger of her left hand which was the bullet-shape of the silver buckle of my belt cinching in my waist tight. Her eyes on me restless as those minnow-sized fish that devour living things in seconds—piranha. Leaned down to ask did I know what the freak time it was and I laughed saying no I did not know what the "freak time" it was, I was sorry. After 10 P.M. I said, this is what I thought the time was up on the ground where there were clocks. This made Plastic Girl laugh too, and a smell of spicy meat came from her opened mouth. She asked didn't I wear a wristwatch?—and I said no, and she laughed again saying Hey was I a girl who didn't give a shit about the time, and I frowned at this, I did not like to hear profanity or nasty words, not even from a girl who stared at me in a way that was flattering. All this while Plastic Girl leaning over me and breathing that meaty smell saying, I guess you're the kind of girl who knows her own mind. That is fucking cool.

Raising her voice to be heard over the racket of the train Plastic Girl started telling me about this place she was expected at, some kind of residence she wasn't going back to, halfway-house, *halfway-to-Hell house*, except somebody there owed her, had clothes of hers and personal documents so she'd have to return except not by any fucking front entrance where you had to sign in, she'd get back inside by a window and it wouldn't be broad fucking daylight, it would be night. I listened to Plastic Girl's voice like it was a radio voice. It was a voice beamed to me that had nothing to do with *me*. Distracted by Plastic Girl's heavy breasts swaying inside the T-shirt, and her belly above the zipper-crotch of the khakis pushing out round and hard like a drum. The bullet-shape silver ring that was *the sign* between us, that (maybe) Plastic Girl had seen also. And the thought came to me *Is this the one? A female?*

But at the next station a swarm of people entered the car. A man pushed between us like Plastic Girl didn't exist. Rude behavior but he was taller and bigger than Plastic Girl and knew she would give him no trouble. Smiling sidelong at me like he knew me, or was pretending to know me, this was a game we'd played before, him and me. (Was it?) A woman seated close by decided to move to another seat, uncomfortable with Plastic Girl and now this new guy hanging above her, each of them drawn to me, as eyes were drawn to me generally, and right away the guy took her place before Plastic Girl could sit down. You could see that Plastic Girl was angry. Baring her teeth like she'd have liked to tear at someone with those teeth. I looked up at her appealing with my eyes, sorry! I was sorry!—but Plastic Girl shrugged and moved off, took a seat farther down the car that had just opened up. As the train lurched I could see her shaved head glowing like a bulb and the platinum-blond quills quivering like antennae. I knew: Plastic Girl would keep her eyes on me, she would not let me go so easily.

The man beside me nudged me—it was the first actual touch of this night, I reacted with a start—asking did I remember him? Huhhh?

Did I remember him? Dunk's the name.

Dunk! I did not remember any *Dunk*.

Laughed to hear such a silly name—*Dunk*.

Sure you do, sweetheart. You remember Dunk.

Then realizing yes I'd met Dunk before. More than once before. Why I'd felt sort of strange seeing him, sort of protected-by-him, the way you do with some individuals, though not with most men, not ever. A few weeks ago we'd got to talking in the subway and he'd taken me for coffee (at Union Square). Possibly I'd been dressed then as I was dressed now. And Dunk in the fake-buckskin jacket he was wearing now, and his steel-gray hair pulled back in a little pigtail at the nape of his neck as it was now. (Had to smile at this little pigtail since Dunk was near-bald except for a band of hair around his bumpy-looking head he'd let grow to pull into a pigtail.) There was something old and comfortable about Dunk, pothead hippie from long ago. Dunk said he remembered me, yes he remembered Lorelei, hey did I know I'd broken his heart? Dunk made a weepy jocular sound like a wheezing heart might make but mostly he was needing to blow his nose which he did in a dirty tissue, making a honking noise so I laughed. That was Dunk's power: to make you laugh. The dirty wadded tissue in his hand was *the sign* for in my pocket was a dirty tissue stained with blood.

Dunk had been a psychiatric social worker for the city. Had to quit after twenty-three years and take disability pay to save his soul, he said. In the coffee shop at Penn Station he told me of his life lapsing into a singsong voice like a lullaby. You could see that Dunk had told his story many times before but Dunk had no other story to tell. He was very lonely, he would confide. His skin exuded heat like a radiator. Made me laugh—(almost)—how his right eye drifted out of focus while his left eye had me pinned. In the coffee shop Dunk paid for my coffee and for something to eat, Dunk believed that I was too skinny. He said that I would never mature if I was malnourished. He said that my organs would age prematurely and that I would die prematurely. He told me of his patient who'd threatened to kill him and he'd said what difference did it make, we're all going to die anyway aren't we. He'd been so depressed. And something terrible had happened to his patient, and Dunk was to blame though no one knew. Though Dunk would not confide in anyone except me.

Then, Dunk said, he got bored with being depressed. I was listening with just half my mind. The other half yearning for *you*. By this time I'd realized that Dunk was not my destiny.

This night, Dunk is asking would I come with him, we could have a meal together. Politely I said thank you, but I have an appointment with someone else.

LORELEI

* * *

Who is my destiny? You?

Whoever it was, I didn't see. Never saw his face. Never saw but a
shadow in the corner of my eye. Great bird spreading its wings. (I
believe it was a man. I am sure it was a man. But even that fact,
I can't be one hundred percent certain of.) At the Fourteenth
Street station. My plan was to take the uptown to Fifty-seventh
Street. Past Times Square. I'd been disappointed in Times Square
lately. The area around Carnegie Hall is very different. Lorelei
would be more visible there. Now standing at the edge of the
platform a little apart from a small crowd gathered for the next
train. A few yards maybe. I didn't believe that I was standing
dangerously close to the edge. Something on the sole of my high-
heeled sandal, something sticky and disgusting like a large wad
of gum. And this gum was like a tongue. Ugh! Trying to scrape
it off my shoe when I saw, or half-saw, your shadow in the corner
of my eye, advancing upon me from the left. The thought came
to me swift and yearning *Please touch me* because it was such a
familiar thought, I did not believe that I was in danger. *Touch
me even if you hurt me. Oh please.*

Then I was falling. I was screaming, and I was falling. It
happened so fast! Faster than I can recount. Though even then
thinking *You touched me at last. It was a human touch. You chose
me because I am beautiful and desirable and young. You chose me
over all the others.*

But already my happiness has ended. I have fallen onto the track. I have fallen helpless, on my back. A smell of oil in my widened nostrils, something musty and cold. Out of nowhere the train is speeding. Oncoming headlights. My body is a boneless rag doll flopping and being crushed by the train. The emergency brakes are thrown but it's too late, it was too late as soon as you moved up stealthily behind me smiling whispering *Lorelei! Lorelei!* in your way of cruel teasing. You pushed me from behind, hard. Swift and hard the palms of your hands flat against my back between my shoulder blades. As if you've planned the act, you've rehearsed the act numerous times to perfection, and in the very act of pushing you are turning aside, to the left, taking care that the momentum of your act doesn't carry you over the edge of the platform and onto the track below with your screaming victim. And you are running, you are pushing past bystanders running and gone with your mysterious cruel smile as below the platform on the tracks inside the terrible grinding wheels my body is caught up, my legs severed at the knees, a wrenching of bone, my left arm is torn off at the shoulder, my skull crushed as you'd crush a bird's egg beneath your careless feet, scarcely knowing you'd crushed it. The silly high-heeled sandals have been tossed from my feet and will be found a dozen yards away. My blood is rushing from my body to congeal with the cold oil and filth of the tracks. My body is crushed, disfigured. You would no longer stare at my beauty. You would no longer recognize Lorelei. On the platform above, strangers are screaming. I want to cry, these strangers care for me. In that instant, they care for me. Fellow passengers who'd disapproved of me in the trains have now forgiven me and are crying Help! Get help! Oh God get help! A tall husky girl who might be Plastic Girl runs to the edge of the platform, can't see me because my body is hidden by the train skidding to a stop.

And Dunk, slack-mouthed in horror. Dunk with his bald-hippie pigtail gone gray. Dunk stunned and sick with grief he has lost me for the final time.

And you others who never knew me except to glimpse a girl pushed in front of a speeding train to her death, these others grieving for me, too. Never knew me in life but will never never forget me as I am in death.

Please love me? My eyes beg. Glancing at the window beside your seat, uptown train flying through the tunnel, lights in the car flickering off, back on, off again and back on like the sensation before sleep. Lights in the car so bright you can't see outside, only your reflection in the grimy window, my own face, and sometimes you don't recognize that face.

Please love me? I love you.

The Rescuer

1.

A call came from home. Your brother, they said.

It was like the crashing fall of a stalactite—a giant stalactite made of ice.

What of my brother, I said. I was the youngest sister of the brood and could not see what any of them had to do with me.

The voice was my father's but funneled through some sort of tunnel- or time-warp. These were people who refused to use cell phones and did not "do" email and their way of communication was the old-fashioned land-phone prominent in their kitchen on its special little table.

"Your brother needs help. He is not well. He refuses to speak to us and will no longer pick up the phone. We have tried and failed as you know. God knows we have tried and failed with Harvey and we are not young any longer. *You* are young, and live close to him."

This was false. This was a lie. I lived at least two hundred miles from Harvey. It was all I could stammer—"No! *You* live closer."

My father explained that Harvey had taken a *leave of absence* from the seminary and was living now in Trenton, New Jersey.

The term *leave of absence* was enunciated with care. There was the wish, on my father's part, that this term not be interpreted as *dropped out, been expelled, failed.*

I had not heard this news. I was stunned and even a little frightened to be told that (1) my brother lived sixty miles from me; (2) my brother had dropped out of the seminary.

My God-besotted brother who was the only person I'd ever heard of who, already in middle school, was convinced that it was his destiny to be a "man of God."

This information was too confusing for me to process. My father continued to speak as my mother, who must have been leaning her ear close to the receiver, spoke also, more forcibly. The overlapping voices made me feel that my brain had split and the two halves were being shaken like chestnuts in a metal container—noise, static, all sense of words lost.

"I can't see Harvey. I—I have no time for—"

"Your poor brother is alone, and you know how innocent and unworldly he is. You know he has 'moods'—'fugues.' Please look in upon him, as you are his sister and our dear daughter. Be kind to him, if you can."

Badly I wanted to break the connection. This was so unfair!

Mercilessly the voices droned on: "And if you could shop for him. And now and then cook a meal for him if you would be so kind . . ."

"I can't. I don't have time. I have my own life now."

"God bless you, dear. If you can do these things for your poor brother, and your parents. We are so helpless here. We are not so well ourselves. We are not so young any longer and already the temperature is so cold at night and the wind whistling through this old house, and the terrible winter looming ahead . . ."

I'd stopped listening. A pounding of blood in my ears drowned out the yammering voices. I muttered *Good night!* and broke the connection.

Will not. Can't make me. No longer. I am not your captive daughter now.

Hurrying on the stairs and talking excitedly to myself and my heel caught in something frayed and suddenly I was plunging forward, downward, headfirst down the remainder of the stairs to strike the hardwood floor and for a stunned moment lying motionless trying to determine if I was alive, or not; if I was conscious, or not; if I'd broken any bones, or stimulated my heart into a wild crazed tachycardia; a chill blackness came over me, like something being swept by a faceless custodian with one of those wide brushy brooms; and someone was shaking my shoulder gently but urgently, a concerned face hovered above mine—*Hello? Are you all right? Let me help you . . .*

One of the young-women residents in Newcomb Hall. A kindly individual with a familiar face though I didn't know her name and now in my deep embarrassment I could only stammer thank you, yes I am all right, I am fine, pressing a wad of tissues against my nose that was leaking blood, thank you *so much.*

Eager to escape! For I could not bear being exposed as clumsy, and pitiable.

Out of the residence hall then, walking swiftly if not very steadily in the cold wet air and I was halfway to my destination when I realized that I'd rushed outside without a coat. Snowflakes melting in my hair, on my eyelashes and warm cheeks.

Leaves stuck to the soles of my feet like sticky tongues. I felt a sing of terror kicking at them.

For a frightening moment I could not recall where I was. Where I was headed. Pulses beat angrily in my head *I am not your captive now!*

I remembered then, I was due at Jester College, one of the University's residential colleges, where the master of the college was hosting a Newcomb Fellows reception. By the time I arrived at the Gothic archway of the master's entrance, my parents' hateful words were dissipated and lost.

In the Graduate College of the University, I was one of eleven Newcomb Fellows. We were four young women and seven young men and we were all graduates of good second-tier universities from which we'd graduated *summa cum laude* and for this reason the great University founded in the eighteenth century, buttressed against financial crises with an endowment of $20 billion, had cast out lifelines to us, to pull us out of the choppy cannibal sea and onto the floating island of the historic University. We were scholars in the humanities and social sciences; our futures shimmered before us like the most seductive of mirages—academic appointments at good universities, freedom to devote to scholar-ship, a commitment to teaching, too—a protected life, utterly enviable. My brother Harvey, older than I by several years, had preceded me into this insulated and protected world; he was a scholar-seminarian, or had been. I was twenty-three and very ambitious. My face was bland as smooth-carved soapstone yet felt to me, from within, like one of those pen-and-ink draw-ings by Matisse of sharp-featured females. My voice was low, murmurous, and gracious; my voice would be described as a distinctly "feminine" voice; if I did not modulate it, my voice would resemble the harsh cracked cry of a famished bird.

At the reception, Newcomb Fellows were introduced to older post-docs and professors in the humanities. At such occasions, I maneuvered myself very well. I am a small light-boned person with a pleasing smile that lights up as automated lights switch on when a human presence approaches. And unobtrusively I made a small evening meal out of the appetizers served at the reception, for I was very frugal, and meant to save money in any way that I could; in my book bag, I secreted away a few extra appetizers wrapped in paper napkins, for midnight when I was likely to be famished.

My scholarly dissertation was to be in the cultural anthro-pology of religion. I was studying with Professor A. who was a world authority on the both the Abrahamic religions of Africa and several indigenous African religions with long histories in the regions now known as Zimbabwe and Sudan. Professor A. had entrusted me with a rare manuscript in the now mostly extinct

Eweian language, which had been several times translated, but never, in Professsor A.'s opinion, accurately; under his guidance, I would translate it, and interpret it.

At the crowded reception I sighted Professor A. across the room. His gaze moved over me, I thought, without recognition; but perhaps the elderly white-haired gentleman had not seen me.

Others were glancing toward me—at my face which was throbbing with heat. A thin trickle of something liquid ran from my nose but I'd captured it in a paper napkin, I'd thought, and blotted it away, before anyone could see.

Someone asked if I'd hurt myself, my eyes and my nose appeared to be bruised. Quickly I denied this. I had not *hurt myself.* I was fine except—a family crisis made it necessary for me to leave the University for a few days, unavoidably.

Family crisis? What was this?

It was utterly shocking to me—my crow-voice, not my soft-modulated feminine voice, had spoken, uttering words I had not meant to speak.

Now I worried that there were blood-drops on my clothes. I could not bring myself to glance downward, to see.

2.

It was a surprise and a shock to see where my brother was living.

The house at 11 Grindell Park did not even look inhabited. It was a weatherworn English Tudor that had once been impressive, you could see—like other, similar houses built in a semi-circle around the derelict park where at the apex of the semi-circle was a small Greek Revival temple that appeared to be a public library, its columns and walls now defaced with graffiti. The park was deserted except for a scattering of homeless individuals who sat, or lay, unmoving as corpses, and dark-skinned boys with pants halfway down their hips as in gangsta films and videos. There were a few others, adult males, who seemed to be arranged like chess pieces, each near-stationary in his own part of the park yet keenly aware, you sensed, of the others. You were made to think of vultures except these were ground-creatures and the storm-damaged trees of the abandoned little urban park would have been too weak to support their weight.

Grindell Park was just inside the Trenton city limits, two blocks from traffic-clogged Camden Avenue. In this part of the city Camden Avenue was a succession of fast-food restaurants, gas stations, and small businesses of which a conspicuous number were shuttered and their properties for rent. Beyond the busy street was a neighborhood of run-down wood frame houses, many of these for rent or abandoned as well. And then there was Grindell Park, another block farther from Camden Avenue, a once-prestigious Trenton neighborhood. It was mystifying to me, as to my parents, why Harvey had moved to Trenton, where he could have known no one; and why to such a neighborhood?

Until now I'd imagined that I knew my brother. I had not always liked him—(to be candid, Harvey hadn't much liked me, or even noticed me)—but I had always admired and envied him and hoped to emulate him in his strategies of escape from our household.

Parked my car at the trash-littered curb in front of 11 Grindell and by the time I removed the key from the ignition the sharp-eyed gangsta boys in the park had already checked it out—secondhand, tarnished, economy-sized, foreign ("Mazda")—and dismissed it.

Still, I locked the doors. My laptop computer was inside, beneath a pile of clothes.

The English Tudor house, once a private home, had been crudely renovated and partitioned into apartments. What must have been an elegant front foyer was now an entryway with a scuffed and soiled tile floor and along one wall a row of cheap aluminum mailboxes.

At a distance of several feet I could recognize Harvey's pinched little block letters—HARVEY SELDEN, APT. 3B.

Two hulking young men in their twenties were descending the stairs, loudly. With them was a large bald dog that, sighting me, began barking hysterically.

The taller of the young men was gripping the dog's chain-leash. Seeing the look of fear in my face he laughed and assured me—"Hey li'l dude, Dargo ain't no danger."

The young man was rail-thin, lanky. His skin was the hue of eggplant, velvety and beautiful. But out of his head sprang fantastical dreadlocks that fell halfway down his back and the way he stared and grinned at me was not comforting.

"You sure you in the right place, li'l dude?"—with a quick canny assessing gaze taking in my pale skin, my facial features. "Come lookin for Mister Selden, is you? He home."

He was laughing at me. Quick-flashing shark-white teeth as he gripped the dog's leash loosely enough so that the dog could lunge at me, as I backed away and cringed.

The dog was pig-shaped, with a pig-snout. Pinched little eyes glaring with rage. It was a pit bull, I thought—bred to attack.

He will not let that dog attack me. Of course he would not.

In my fright and confusion I had no more than a blurred impression of a third person, an older man, in the gloom of the first-floor landing, who'd been following the young men and calling after them on their thunderous descent down the stairs. It might have been that the young men had taken something from the man he hadn't wanted to give them but they were so openly derisive and playful, they didn't seem like thieves.

As I cringed back against the row of cheap mailboxes the dreadlock-boy allowed the incensed Dargo to stand on his hind legs and snap and bite at me, so close I felt the dog's hot spittle on my hands, which I'd raised to protect my face.

The other youth was shorter, and heavier; his skin was sallow, his eyes pinched and his face curiously flat like a sea-creature that is all spherical face, with frontal eyes. His grin was strained and elated as if he'd have liked his friend to release Dargo but he kept a formal distance between us, half-hiding behind the dreadlock-boy who was smirking and teasing: "He you' brother is he, hey? Girl, that be some *bro-ther*."

I had no idea what this jeering remark meant. The young man was combative and self-possessed and spoke in a fluent, fluid, mocking way, like a rap artist; on the right side of his handsome face was a tattoo, savage yet symmetrical. Seeing how he'd frightened me he relented, "Yo, damn dog!"—yanking Dargo away.

The two youths were loud-laughing and contemptuous slamming out the front door. I was trembling badly: Dargo's spittle was cooling on my hands.

Whoever had been on the first-floor landing hadn't seemed to see me cowering in fear below, or hadn't cared to see. He'd retreated and disappeared from view.

Had it been Harvey? I seemed to know, yes it was.

I knocked on the door of 3B. Inside there was silence, as of an indrawn breath.

"Hello? Harvey? It's . . . me."

I lifted my fist to knock again, a little louder, and the door was suddenly opened, and there my brother Harvey stood before me, a look of astonishment on his face.

Astonishment and something else—dismay, disapproval.

"Lydia? What are you . . ."

Harvey blinked and squinted behind me, toward the stairs. I thought *He is disappointed. He expected the boys to return.*

In our mutual surprise we stared at each other. Here was something strange: Harvey was shorter than I remembered him.

My brother had always been tall and lanky, since he'd been a young teenager. By the age of twenty he'd been at least six feet tall. But now, he couldn't have been more than five feet eight or nine. (The last I'd had my height checked, I was about five feet six.) And Harvey was thinner, almost sickly. His narrow jaws were covered in stubble and his eyes, always mournful and brooding, were threaded with broken capillaries.

Harvey appeared to be only partly dressed. Soiled jeans, an undershirt, no shoes and no socks.

I tried to explain, *They* had sent me.

Harvey would know who *they* were who'd sent me to look after him and also to spy on him for their sake.

(I had called my parents back, to get Harvey's address. Why I had capitulated to their unjust demand I will never know.)

(All of what followed from that act was nothing I had wished for myself and yet somehow, it seemed to be unfolding as in a script written by a malicious stranger, in opposition to my deepest desire.)

Harvey was in a state of such nerves, I had to repeat what I'd said. He kept glancing behind me, peering down at the foyer below. Outside, the dog's hysterical barking had faded; the boys were gone.

Dismayed Harvey stared at me, his youngest sister. He'd have liked to simply shut the door—shut it in my face—but instead he sighed, and relented, inviting me inside.

"Since you're here, Lydia."

* * *

He is not happy to see me. Of course, this is a stupid mistake.

I stepped inside the apartment. I glanced furtively about the room—a high-ceilinged dimly lit space containing mismatched shabby furniture, boxes and cartons and stacks of books and a badly scuffed hardwood floor. The windows were without curtains or blinds. The overhead light was a bare bulb of about sixty watts. It might have been a hotel room in a cheap welfare hotel.

Harvey was very distracted. Though he tried to talk to me, and to listen to me, clearly his mind was elsewhere; he was alert to every sound in the house, and on the street; a muscle twitched in his unshaven jaws and his bloodshot eyes seemed without focus. He failed to invite me to sit down. He failed to offer me anything—even a glass of water.

There was a discomfiting smell in the place—something acrid, fermented, gassy. And beneath, a prevailing odor of dirty laundry, unwashed flesh.

Gamely I tried to explain another time why I'd come, why my parents had sent me. I did not tell Harvey that I was on a mission to "help" him—that would have been insulting to his pride.

My brother had always been proud. Vain of his high grades, his "good-boy" reputation. Adults had admired him. Less so, people his own age.

"Father and Mother would have come to see you themselves," I said, unconvincingly, "except—it's so far for them to drive, and they're—old . . . not well . . ."

My parents were not old, really: scarcely in their sixties. Not *old.*

Nor were they unwell, so far as I knew. Despite what they'd said on the phone.

All this while Harvey was trying clumsily to hide something in his hand. Trying to divert my attention he maneuvered himself to a table in a corner of the room, where he shoved whatever he'd been holding—(a small package or bag?)—beneath a pile of newspapers.

By degrees Harvey regained a measure of his old composure. He'd gotten over the shock and something of the displeasure of seeing me in the corridor outside his door and spoke to me in the voice of an elder brother giving advice to his naïve and intrusive sister: "Jesus, Lydia! You shouldn't have come here. Our parents have nothing to do with my life any longer—they are the only bond between us, and that bond has been broken. They know this, and you should know it, too. You should not be their *handmaid*." He paused, wiping furiously at his nose. He'd worked himself up to a kind of anger. "I guess you can stay the night, then drive back tomorrow to—wherever you came from."

Surely Harvey must have known where I was in graduate school, at which distinguished University, quite as distinguished as the seminary he'd quit, and so this was some sort of brotherly insult, I supposed. I tried not to feel hurt. I tried not to reveal hurt.

"If that's what you want, Harvey. But I think . . ."

"Yes. It is what I want. Haven't you been listening, for Christ's sake!"

In Harvey's presence, inevitably I was cast back into the pitiable role of *baby sister*—an object of bemused affection, or affable contempt. My sisters had sometimes liked me, and sometimes not; not often, my older siblings had time for me. Now Harvey said, coldly: "Our parents have no right to interfere in my life—or in yours. This is not a safe environment for a girl like you."

I thought *But what about you?*

For it seemed to me, in the dimly lighted room, that was badly cluttered as a storage room with boxes (unpacked books and papers) on the floor, and scattered white plastic bags underfoot, that something was wrong with my brother: part of his face was missing.

Harvey's hair was long and unkempt, falling to his shoulders, but at the crown of his head he was beginning to go bald. The effect was eerie—as if someone had grabbed his long hair and tugged it partway back his head.

For as long as I could remember Harvey wore his dull-brown hair conventionally cut, trimmed at the sides and back. He'd dressed neatly, inconspicuously. If he was to be a "man of God" it was not as a fervid Evangelist preacher but as a scholarly theologian like his hero Reinhold Niebuhr. He'd never smoked, never drank, so far as anyone in the family knew; he'd never been involved with girls or women, and had had few friends. He'd never appeared in my sight so altered, so—disheveled. It was as if a giant hand had snatched up poor Harvey and shaken him, hard. His skin was both sallow and red-mottled as if he were very warm; his hair hung in his face, in greasy strands. He wore soiled jeans and a soiled T-shirt. In college and at the seminary he'd worn proper white shirts, ties, and jackets; he'd acquired a settled yet expectant look as of middle age, while in his early twenties. My parents had proudly shown photographs of their only son studying at the distinguished seminary at which Reinhold Niebuhr had himself taught fifty years before. *Our son is studying to be a man of God!*

Such silly boastfulness was typical of my parents. Perhaps it is typical of all parents. I did not feel envy for Harvey, only resentment and frustration.

When I did well in school, my parents seemed scarcely to notice.

Good work Lydia. Very good.

There is a finite supply of love in a family, perhaps. By the time the youngest child arrives, that supply has diminished.

Harvey was complaining: "You don't seem to understand, Lydia, that this part of Trenton is an environment in which a—a person—like you—will be singled out for the wrong kind of attention. You will be *singular*. You're a young Caucasian woman, you're attractive, you're alone, and you are vulnerable." *Attractive* and *vulnerable* were uttered accusingly. *Alone* seemed to me unfair.

"But I'm not alone. I'm with you."

Harvey stared at me, offended.

"You are not *with me*. You've just intruded, uninvited. And you're leaving, tomorrow."

I saw that Harvey's hands were trembling. His fingernails were ragged. He looked at least ten years older than his age. We had not embraced in a greeting—we hadn't brushed lips against the other's cheek—but I was aware of my brother's fierce breath like something combustible. The thought came to me *Oh God—he's sick. He's a drug addict.* I didn't wish to think that my brother might be paying those hulking youths to service him in ways other than just supplying drugs.

In a bitter voice Harvey continued to complain about our parents intruding in his life, and how little they understood of his life. He'd worked himself up into a state in which he was cursing the seminary as well—a "Protestant refuge against reality." In a voice heavy with sarcasm he spoke of individuals whose names meant little to me, professors of his at the seminary.

The seminary was one of the oldest and most distinguished seminaries in the United States, overlooking the Hudson River just north of New York City. It had been a great honor for Harvey to receive an appointment as a fellow at this seminary after his graduation from college; my parents had boasted of nothing else for months. But now, Harvey seemed to be expressing contempt for it.

I was waiting for Harvey to suggest that we go downstairs to my car, and bring my things into his apartment—my hastily packed suitcase, a backpack and my laptop. But he didn't seem to think of it. I couldn't help thinking *He is waiting for me to be discouraged, and to leave.*

It was then I saw: Harvey's left ear had been injured. It looked mangled as if it had been partly bitten off and was covered in ugly dark scabs, all but hidden by his straggly hair.

"Harvey, what happened to you? My God."

"What—where?" Laughing irritably Harvey tried to pass off my alarm as some curious foible of my own.

"Your ear. Here." Gingerly, I meant to touch the mangled ear but Harvey pushed my hand away.

"There's nothing wrong with my ear. Jesus!" Harvey's sallow face was flushed with embarrassment. I remembered how, as a child, usually a very well behaved boy, Harvey would suddenly flare up in anger if one of our sisters teased him a little too long or made a gesture to touch him.

I remembered the lanky-limbed "good" boy striking out with his fists. Kicking.

He turned on me, furious. It was the first time since I'd stepped into his apartment that Harvey had actually looked at *me*.

"What about you? It looks like somebody blackened your eyes. Your face is bruised. What the hell happened to *you*?"

I'd forgotten my accident entirely. My face was more or less numb, and no longer throbbed with pain.

"I—I had an accident. I slipped on a staircase, and . . ."

Harvey clearly disbelieved me; nor did my explanation sound very plausible, even to me.

"I wasn't *beaten*."

"Well. I wasn't beaten, either."

"But your ear looks mutilated. Part of the lobe is missing . . ."

Harvey ran his fingers rapidly over the scarred ear. "It was an accident, too. Dargo mistook me for someone else."

113

"That horrible dog? He attacked you?"

"Leander—that's Dargo's master—wasn't to blame. Leander wouldn't hurt *me*. But it was a confused scene, there was a lot going on and the dog got confused. Such things happen, in Grindell Park."

Wryly, Harvey rubbed the scabby ear. And then I saw that the tip of his little finger was missing, too, on his right hand.

3.

A night passed, and another day, and a night. Harvey was gentlemanly enough to lend me his bed—but such a lumpy, smelly bed, with grungy bedclothes and a pillow that looked as if it had been flattened with a baseball bat; when I asked Harvey for clean sheets he laughed at me and said the God damn sheets would be cleaned when someone took the laundry to the Laundromat, how else?

I thought this was probably an invitation, in my brother's oblique way, to take the laundry to a Laundromat for him; to stay a while longer, and be of help.

Of course, Harvey would never have appealed to me directly.

So I drove to the nearest Laundromat, which was on Camden Avenue a half-mile away. There was a grocery store close by so I set out for the store while Harvey's laundry was being washed.

And there on the sidewalk was Leander taller and more savage-looking in sunlight, half his face a lurid tattoo and dreadlocks falling down his back.

"Hiya li'l dude. How's it goin."

I was trying not to acknowledge him, not to see him. Except of course Leander recognized me and knew exactly who I was.

The relief was, Leander didn't have the pig-pit-bull with him, straining at the leash. It seemed strange to see him alone on the sidewalk, not unlike an ordinary pedestrian. He said, in a mock-accusing voice: "Y'know—you' brother owes somebody a sum. He told you this, eh? Like six hundred eighty-eight dollars the fucker owe. You will pay, eh?"

"I will pay—why?"

"You brother say you are here to help him. You here to get him well again. He love you, he say. My sister is the one of all the world, I love."

Leander spoke extravagantly. His speech was a kind of music. What he said was unbelievable but he spoke with such sincerity, you wanted to believe. As if it were Harvey and not Leander who spoke: Harvey the young idealist and not the burnt-out Harvey who was now.

"Well. I love Harvey, too."

"There you go, girl! That be good for both."

The dark-skinned boy loomed over me smiling and twitching his lips that were thick, protuberant. As his eyes were protuberant, like the eyes of a primitive African carving. The tattoo looked painted-on, savage; it appeared to be a copy of the Maori tribal tattoo that the ex-heavyweight champion Mike Tyson had had tattooed on half his face. Leander's breath, too, was fierce—combustible. Heat lifted from his oily-dark skin, where he'd left partway open a smart black suede coat that fell to his knees; beneath the coat, he was wearing just a suede vest and a gold chain.

I said I didn't have so much money. I said I was a student, like my brother.

Leander said, sneering, "You too old, be a student! Fuck that bullshit, man! Neither of you, specially *him*. Ain't be any asshole gon believe you be *students* of—what?"

"I am a—a graduate student—cultural anthropology—"

"Cuntchural 'pology—bull*shit*. Like you' brother sayin he gon be some kinda preacher. Is that fucked, man! He owe us this sum six hundred ninety-eight dollars, man. It goin up all the time, man—'int'rest.' He say you come here, gon help him out."

"But I—I don't have six hundred dollars . . ."

In fact, of course I did have six hundred dollars. I had somewhere beyond sixteen hundred dollars, in a banking account near the University.

This was my fellowship, or rather part of it. Monthly installments were wired to the account, not much, but enough to cover my expenses month to month. I had to suppose that Harvey too had such an arrangement at the seminary, or had had such an arrangement before he'd dropped out.

Leander leaned close to me as if he could read my thoughts. I felt a sensation of faintness, quickness of breath. I thought *He can't hurt me here in front of witnesses.*

Yet—were there "witnesses" on Camden Avenue? Traffic moving in an erratic stream of stops and starts—a predominance of vans, trucks, buses—a scattering of dark-skinned individuals waiting at a bus stop—a few grim-faced pedestrians. In this part of Trenton, no one dallied: everyone had a mission, to get somewhere else. If Leander threatened me, or attacked me, would anyone so much as glance in my direction? Would anyone *care*?

He was laughing at me. Between us there was a bond of some kind: as if we'd known each other in the past, intimately.

The Maori tattoo: an eerie curdled-cream-color, bracketing half his face like sharks' teeth.

"He say you' name is—*Lyd-jai?* You gon be my friend, girl— you see. There's ways of payin back what you' brother owe, we work out just fine betwin us, *Lyd-jai*."

These were ominous words. I did not quite hear these words. I did hear *Lyd-jai*. Harvey must have spoken with Leander just recently, without my knowledge, telling Leander my name.

Leander reached out to touch my face—to frame my face in his hands. His movements were snaky-quick, I had no time to pull away.

Long fingers framing my face, a pressure of thumbs at the corners of my eyes.

"You be pretty-girl, you' eyes some kinda *blue*—like sky. But not Trenton sky."

Leander spoke with a mocking sort of tenderness. I stood very still, not breathing, just slightly on my toes, as he was pulling upward at my head, straining my neck.

He leaned his savage smiling face to mine. His nostrils were enormous. And the dark-purplish lips enormous. At the corners of my eyes, the pressure of his fingers tightened. I tried not to panic thinking *He could gouge out my eyes. He could snap my neck. He is restraining himself.*

Instead, Leander stooped and took hold of my lower lip in his teeth. It wasn't a kiss—it was a bite: a quick sharp nasty bite of my lower lip.

Then, a sudden release.

Laughter in my face, and release.

Dazed, I stumbled away. I managed to find a tissue in my handbag, to press against my bleeding mouth.

At first I wasn't sure if it was blood that I was tasting, or saliva that seemed to be flooding my mouth.

If he is infected. HIV, AIDS.

I walked away—no one on the street seemed to have noticed Leander and me.

Or, if anyone had noticed, he had not intervened.

I was headed for—where?—a grocery store. Pinneo's Market: a corner store with a small littered parking lot.

Possibly Leander was watching me, hands on his hips, standing behind me. Or maybe he'd disappeared.

Grocery store!—food store! There was virtually no food in Harvey's refrigerator. I recalled my parents enjoining me to shop for Harvey, cook for him, make sure that he ate . . . But I had to feed myself, too. By mid-morning of this first full day in Trenton, I was ravenously hungry.

In the little grocery store, which looked to be very old, family-owned, smelling of Mediterranean spices, cloves of raw garlic, black olives, I pushed a rickety cart along narrow, congested aisles of mostly canned goods. Out of nowhere a boldly bright girl of about nineteen, with toffee-colored skin, and dyed-cranberry hair in stiff cornrows, approached me. At first I thought she worked in the store, then I saw that she was a customer, or had followed me inside.

"Say, girl—that my cousin L'nd'r I saw you just now talking with. Girl, I wouldn't."

"Wouldn't—what?"

"Wouldn't hang out none with L'nd'r. That be a mistake. Get too close with that type, y'know? L'nd'r no common cit'zen."

The girl's smile was a sneering sort of smile, yet not unfriendly. She was a gorgeous young woman of about my height, much fleshier than I was, with thick crimson lips and heavily made-up eyes like a model in a rap-music video.

"Girl, you hearin me? You lookin kinda—lost. What you got to know is, my cousin L'nd'r is not one for trifling."

"He—he's a friend of my brother's . . ."

The girl laughed as if I'd said something witty.

"Girl, he ain't no friend of any *brother*. Believe me, girl. You better run-like-hell in some other direction from L'nd'r is what I'm saying."

"Thank you. I will 'run-like-hell' when Leander comes near, I *promise*."

The girl laughed. She introduced herself as Maralena. I meant to continue shopping but she followed close after me.

"There's no good buyin 'fresh produce' in any store like this. It's all old-stuff, see. You get it home, it's goin brown. Just get like can-things, bottle-things, like that. Freezer-things, you got to check the date. He put the old crap up front, the new stuff at the back. You got to use your thinking, a place like this. He gonna cheat you he see you some white-girl dropped by ain't gon be a steady customer."

I felt a sensation of warmth for Maralena. She looked nothing like her dark-skinned cousin but she was as exotic as he with her beautifully cornrowed hair and glamorous eyes. She smelled strongly of something fruity, sweet—hair pomade? Her mouth was swollen-looking as if it had been vigorously kissed and sucked.

She wore clothes in layers. Long-sleeved black T-shirt over a tight little black short-sleeved T-shirt. Tight black skirt that barely covered her buttocks and beneath thin black leggings and black boots to the knee.

I'd placed a few items in the rickety cart. Pasta in a cardboard box, cans of "spaghetti" sauce. Boxes of cereal. A jar of applesauce, a quart container of yogurt, a container of vitamin D–fortified milk. And cans of condensed soup. At the checkout counter I hoped Maralena would have gone away but there she was waiting for me, checking her cell phone. When she moved her head, the cornrowed plaits rippled.

"I better walk you to you' car, girl. Maybe come along, you goin to Grindell Park. Don't want nobody hittin on you."

4.

Why are you here. Why living in such a place.

What are these people to you. Harvey, answer me!

But Harvey shrugged off my questions. Harvey seemed scarcely aware of his surroundings. Of his old life as a seminary student he'd brought few clothes, books in boxes scattered about the apartment, folders of manuscript drafts, notes, and photocopied texts. (The texts were in languages unknown to me—extinct languages like Aramaic, Attic Greek, Koine Greek, Sanskrit and Latin.) Often Harvey hid away in his bedroom—(a squalid room he needn't have forbade me to enter, one glance inside was enough to dissuade me)—working on translations of certain of these texts, or on his own "private" project.

This was encouraging, I thought. Harvey was still connected with his scholarly work; he had not given up entirely.

"Certainly I haven't *quit*. I never *quit*. I am in a kind of *suspended time,* that's all."

"But—is it an official leave? Does your advisor know where you are? Are you still getting money from your fellowship?"

"I refuse to be interrogated," Harvey said coldly. "Worry about your own fellowship."

Several times, I begged Harvey to share with me what he was working on. To read to me, for instance, a passage of Biblical Aramaic, which I had never heard read aloud, and then to translate it for me.

"No. Not possible."

"But why not?"

"I said *no*."

"But—I'm interested in Aramaic. In the cosmology of the Hebrew Bible. My work with the Eweian text, the theme of the 'creation of the world and of the first man and woman'— all those instances of 'sacred births'—I'm very interested, Harvey."

"You don't know enough to be 'interested' in my subject."

Coldly and cruelly my brother spoke. But then, a moment later, I saw that his creased face shone with tears.

He'd begun to forget, he told me. His knowledge of ancient languages was "leaking" from his brain. He had to work many times longer at translating just a passage, than he'd worked a year ago . . . Sometimes he couldn't recognize a word and when he looked it up in a dictionary he saw that it was a common word, one he knew well.

I persuaded Harvey to show me the photocopied text which he was trying to translate and of course it was incomprehensible to me. Yet, like the musical cadences of Leander's and Maralena's speech, fascinating.

Codes to be decoded. Secrets to be revealed.

Just to acknowledge the forbidden mystery. To approach it.

There was a room in Harvey's apartment that must have been at one time a child's room. A nursery.

A small room overlooking, at a little distance, desolate Grindell Park where drug dealers and their customers did business through daylight hours and well into twilight when their furtive and unvarying figures dissolved into night.

Take the room, no one's using it, Harvey said. He'd given up expecting me to leave.

I had given up expecting to leave, for the time being.

For I was shopping now for Harvey, and preparing meals for him, as for myself.

I was able to work in these new surroundings, I'd discovered. A curious thrill came over me opening my familiar Eweian text in this new place, spreading out my papers, translator's dictionary, drafts. Harvey's apartment was not wired and so I could work on my computer only as a word processor; but if I wanted to do research on the Internet, I could take the laptop to the Grindell Park library which was open for limited hours three days a week, and plug it in there.

My room I swept, cleaned. There was even a table to serve as a desk and another, lower table, upon which I could spread my things.

Noises in the street, or on Camden Avenue, or in the park were not distracting as one might think. At the University, voices in the apartment beneath mine, or on the stairs, or the sound of music at a little distance were very annoying to me, as incursions on my privacy and my need to concentrate; here in Trenton, it came to be silence that was disconcerting for it is silence that precedes the most jarring noises.

In the distance, gunshots. More than once, I'd heard.

Leander and his flat-faced friend Tin—(I think that was the improbable name: *Tin*)—sometimes dropped by the apartment unannounced. And sometimes, with them Maralena.

At the window-table I sat staring. I was strangely calm, though apprehensive. If a script was being prepared it was not a script I could decipher, as I could not decipher Biblical Aramaic, and scarcely Eweian. Fantasies came to me as I stared at rainwater spilling out of a gutter beside the window, streaming black rain on a steep roof spilling out and falling in a noisy cascade, water losing its transparency and turning to blood. I thought *Harvey would not save me. I must save myself.*

"Help me, Lydia! I th-think I need help . . ."

My brother's skin was ashen. His teeth were chattering.

Like bones rattling loosely in a tight taut envelope of skin his teeth were chattering audibly and he was leaning on me weak-kneed soon as I'd returned from working in the Grindell Park library—(one of the branch library's few patrons, at a table still bright-polished as if it had not been used much in recent years and an object of some smiling attention from the sole white middle-aged female librarian)—and out of a heap of bedclothes and towels on the floor of his bedroom I found a ratty blanket to pull over him as he lay shuddering in the lumpy-mattressed bed. For the past eighteen hours Harvey had been remote and irritable and when I'd returned from the library with my laptop he had not unlocked the door for some minutes so I'd pressed my ear to the door listening jealously *Are they there? Leander, Maralena?*—but when finally Harvey stumbled to the door to open it he was alone, so terribly alone, my brother who'd once been a tall handsome bookish man now inches shorter and one of his bony shoulders higher than the other and his hair disheveled, his breath fierce as gasoline, staggering as I bore his weight into the dank bedroom, onto the dank bed, and if someone had been in the apartment with him there was no trace remaining except a smell of something acrid and harsh, had they been smoking hashish?—a jealous thought came to me as I shook down the thermometer, unexpectedly discovering a thermometer in Harvey's very dirty bathroom in a corroded medicine cabinet above the badly stained sink; though I knew relatively little of first aid, as of anything practical in our lives, I did know that a sudden spike in temperature possibly signaling an infection often presented as convulsive shivering. And so I shook the thermometer down to 96°F, then inserted it beneath my brother's tongue that looked pale with slime, held the thermometer in place as Harvey continued to shiver and shudder and when at last I could read the thermometer the little red column of mercury indicated a temperature of 100.2 degrees. This was not dangerously high, yet—was it?—I wasn't sure. Swaths of Harvey's body were hot to the touch yet other parts clammy-cold. I gave him a double-strength Tylenol and brought him glasses of water insisting that he drink for he must not become dehydrated—(if he was taking drugs, a possible side effect might be dehydration, constipation)—and through the long night I watched over him at his bedside as he slept fitfully amid noises from the street, car engines and door-slammings and shouts, drunken laughter, in the distance the now-familiar sounds of gunfire—single shots, repeated shots—wailing sirens like maddened confetti illuminating the nighttime sky above the doomed city of Trenton; closer by, the seething life of Grindell Park which was more populated by night than by day though invisible in the night for which I felt an irrational envy, and yearning; for my labor with the Eweian manuscript was so very slow, painstakingly slow as if I were pushing a small bean across a tilted floor with my nose, craven and abashed and utterly broken-backed pushing this tiny black bean with my nose while all around me was a rich and unfathomable life unknown and unnameable by one like myself. *Some white-girl ain't gon be a steady customer.*

Harvey moaned in his sleep. Tossed and flung his limbs in his sleep. I wondered what drug he'd taken, what Leander was selling him—cocaine?—heroin?—or maybe Harvey wasn't using drugs but was self-infected, the toxins in his body now concentrated, gaining strength. Near dawn his forehead didn't feel so scalding-hot to my touch and he seemed to have ceased sweating, though his T-shirt and boxers were damp with sweat and smelled of his body. And now near dawn the jarring seductive unfathomable noises of the night were subsiding. A sound of heavy truck-traffic on Camden Avenue, signaling a new day. And even the sirens had subsided. For all who were to be taken to the ER, or the Mercer County morgue, or to one or another of the city's detention facilities, had now been taken, and admitted. And I thought how easy life is for those who merely live it without hoping to understand it; without hoping to "decode," classify and analyze it; without hoping to acquire a quasi-invulnerable meta-life which is the life of the mind and not the triumphant life of the body. Breathe in, breathe out. My lower lip throbbed in recalled surprise, pain. Yet I had not recoiled from the pain. *You gon be my friend—you see. There's ways of paying back what you' brother owe.*

In the morning Harvey recalled little of the night. Laughing wryly as if he'd had some kind of hangover—"Metaphysical, felt like."

On the table we used for meals, in a corner of the living room, I'd placed for him a bowl of Cheerios, a small container of yogurt, a pitcher of milk and a half-grapefruit from Pinneo's that wasn't yet overripe. Harvey's mouth moved as if he were unable to speak. He stared unshaven, red-eyed and barefoot and his hair straggling in his face. He had pulled off the sweat-soaked underwear in which he'd slept but he had not showered, only just pulled on T-shirt and boxers from the bureau drawer of recently laundered underwear I'd established for him. He muttered something that resembled *Thank you Lydia. Thank you for my life.*

The (very dirty) bathroom—(corroded) medicine cabinet—stained sink, stained toilet bowl, stained linoleum floor—holding my breath and my nostrils pinched I managed to clean, scrub, even polish to a degree with Dutch Cleanser, Windex, mangled sponges and paper towels.

*   *   *

He had an addiction, he confessed.

Scattered about the apartment were ghostly white plastic bags imprinted BOOK BAZAAR, I'd been noticing since I'd first stepped into the apartment.

A secondhand bookstore on State Street, downtown Trenton. He'd made "raids" on Book Bazaar he said, since he'd first discovered it.

I'd noticed of course: in stacks on windowsills and any available surfaces were battered-looking books, some of them hardcover and many paperback; some of them looking as if they'd been left in the rain, and left to dry in the sun; some of them with titles like *Sacred Texts of the Hebrew Bible, Intertextuality in Ezekiel, A History of the Religions of Late Antiquity, The Formation of the Hebrew Bible,* and some with such titles as *Visions of Hell, An Anatomy of the Apocalypse, The Millennium Comics, Ballads of Heaven and Hell, Was Jesus Gay? Jesus' Son.* These were recent purchases intended to supplement Harvey's older scholarly texts which he'd brought in boxes to Grindell Park, yet unpacked.

An addiction, Harvey said. Like a sickness.

(Not an addiction I'd expected Harvey to confess though I didn't tell him that.)

For only books could help, Harvey believed. The human predicament.

Human predicament?

Human *fate*.

I remembered from our childhood that Harvey was always reading—and writing. Always my older brother had felt that the next book he picked up might be *the book* to change his life and always he was disappointed—to a degree. There was the Holy Bible—he'd naively believed to be the word of God until he'd begun studying the history of the Hebrew Bible in college— one of those courses cunningly titled The Bible as Literature. Still, Harvey believed that the Bible contained great riches, to be properly decoded. Books provided not only histories of the world but also wisdom to help with one's personal life; even, in his particular circumstances, if he was lucky, with his Aramaic translation. So, he said, he was always *trolling* at the secondhand bookstore to see what might change his life.

He had a friend at Book Bazaar, he said. His only *true friend* in Trenton.

Harvey went on to say that books were the soul of human civilization and that a civilization without books would lose its soul. All that was significant had already been written and was waiting to be read, Harvey said.

The more ancient the text, the closer to the source of Truth.

The more recent the text, the farther from the source of Truth.

In the past several decades since the advent of the Internet, things are ever more swiftly flattening and thinning, Harvey said. You could acquire vast quantities of data but could not recall it after five minutes. You could process such data through your brain only with difficulty. The human brain was (de)volving, with each generation. It was like pouring water on an actual, exposed brain—most of the water just runs off. A few minuscule puddles might be retained but that's it.

Harvey was one to talk! Missing part of an ear, a finger, and more recently his right leg had begun to seem shorter than the left.

One day, I drove downtown to Book Bazaar on State Street.

How disappointing Trenton was! I had anticipated an interesting old "historic" city, landmark buildings, churches—instead, the city center seemed to have undergone an urban renewal of such perfunctory architectural design, or lack of design, that there remained not a single building of interest; all were functional, unattractive storefronts, slickly synthetic as a cheap stageset. But 2291 State Street was at the edge of the city center in a yet-unbulldozed neighborhood of older buildings: basement, first, second, and third floors crammed with books.

Old books, many-times-sold books, battered books, wetted-and-dried books, a repository of strangers' dreams to be decoded.

There appeared to be just one clerk in the store—a youngish man in his thirties with his hair in a ponytail, receding hairline like Harvey's and wire-rimmed glasses like Harvey's glasses; within seconds of greeting me, he told me his name: "Wystan." ("My parents named me for W. H. Auden. They were both English majors at Rutgers. Except now it's just a weird name no one has ever heard of.") Wystan wore cargo pants low on his narrow hips and a baggy black T-shirt imprinted with BOOK BAZAAR in red letters. Something glinted at his left ear—a little gold stud.

Wystan stared at me with a peculiar little smile. Eagerly he followed me along the cramped aisles chattering and asking questions. I had the impression that he was lonely: very likely, few customers came into Book Bazaar and very few who looked like me—that is, like a graduate student at a good university, and white-skinned. When Wystan asked who I was, he wasn't discouraged; with the air of one accustomed to rebuffs he simply changed his tact, and took up other subjects. He boasted to me that one of his duties was to comb through "estate libraries"—cartons of books stored in the basement—he "siphoned off" the very best books—first editions, copies signed by authors like Carl Sandburg, Edna St. Vincent Millay, Glenway Wescott, Isaac Asimov, Pearl Buck and H. L. Mencken. Once, he'd found a first edition of *Innocents Abroad* signed with a scrawled signature—just legible as *Mark Twain*.

"Did you sell it?" I asked; and Wystan said, snorting in horror, "*Sell* it? Christ, no! It's the gem of my personal collection."

Adding, in a lowered voice, "And another gem—a first edition of Raymond Chandler's *The Lady in the Lake*."

"Really! That must be quite a collector's item, too. Where did you get it?"

Wystan smiled slyly, waggling his fingers to suggest that he'd—possibly—stolen it.

"Oh but—from where?" I tried not to sound shocked or disapproving.

"A 'mystery bookshop' in Tribeca. It wasn't easy, such a precious first edition wouldn't be on an open shelf, but—there are ways, if you're a book-person and in the trade."

I wondered why Wystan was telling me such things that did not reflect well upon him. I wondered if they could be true.

I wondered what Wystan did with his collection. I could not imagine that his living quarters were very safe, if anywhere near this shabby Trenton neighborhood.

"I sleep with my collection, virtually," Wystan said, as if reading my thoughts. "My special books are in a bookcase beside my bed, and I've arranged a system of strings and little bells, that would alert me if someone tried to take a book."

"But when you're gone, during the day?"

Wystan frowned. "When I'm gone from a place, it shifts out of focus. It becomes background. I can't be distracted by thinking of it. But I do have locks and bolts on windows and a double lock on the door of my apartment."

Then, a moment later, "Maybe you'll see my collection, some day."

To this startling suggestion, I could not think of any polite reply.

I worried that Wystan's employer might overhear him, his voice was so squeaky-strident, but Wystan couldn't help bragging and making me laugh.

Next, he tried to talk me into coming into the basement with him—"Just to see what a 'book mausoleum' is like"—but I resisted. Not that I feared Wystan so much as I feared the airlessness of such a space. With a lurid sort of zest Wystan described to me how he had to crawl along the floor in certain parts of the ("not always dry") basement, or clamber and crawl on top of the stacked cartons; he saw ghostly movements in the corners of his eyes and heard whispers and laughter; he even smelled hair oil, he claimed, of "another era." Yet, he insisted adamantly he "did not succumb" to such ghosts. He did not "believe" in ghosts—"Do you?"

"No! What a silly question."

"Good. We have in common the rationalist's belief in *this world only.*"

How appealing Wystan was, in his clumsy way. He reminded me of my brother when Harvey was being sweet and charming and not sarcastic or mean to me—a rarity.

And I saw that Wystan was attracted to me. The curious way he peered at my face.

Maybe noting my swollen lower lip, that had been bitten and bloodied.

Gallantly Wystan helped me carry some of the books I'd selected from Religion/Anthropology shelves. (Lesser-known titles by Margaret Mead, Gregory Bateson, and Clifford Geertz; provocatively titled trade paperbacks *Totem, Taboo and Mother-Child Rituals in Africa,* and *A Cultural History of Infanticide,* grimy mass-market paperbacks on many topics including, for Harvey, *Kierkegaard, Hegel, and Unbelief* and *Forbidden and Denied: Apocryphal Books of the Bible* as well as a half-dozen back issues of *Journal of Early Christian Studies.*) Each time I selected a book to buy, Wystan marveled at my "judicious taste." His feeling for me, a mysterious young Caucasian woman who was clearly well educated, who'd entered the run-down secondhand

Book Bazaar out of nowhere on a weekday morning, was touchingly clumsy as an oversized beach ball Wystan was obliged to carry in his arms, unable to pass on to another, or to set aside. For a dreamy hour I wandered the aisles of the store feeling as Harvey claimed to feel—that somewhere in all these thousands of books there was a singular book that would speak intimately to me, and change my life—but where was it?

Or maybe, I'd bought it.

Finally I told Wystan that I had to leave.

"So soon? You haven't seen the third floor—sci-fi, dark fantasy, poetry, women's studies, gay and lesbian, New Age."

"Thank you. But I have to leave."

"The basement! The 'book mausoleum' that contains unknown treasures . . ."

"Thank you, Wystan. Not today."

"Next time, then! That's a promise."

Clearly there was no one else in the store, since it was Wystan who checked out my books at the cashier's counter. In his eagerness to stay at my side he'd ignored another, single, male customer who'd drifted in, and out, of the store without a purchase.

My precious armload of paperback books came to just thirty-two dollars and ninety-eight cents. This, I paid with cash, but Wystan pressed me to give him my address so that Book Bazaar could send out notices of store events and sales—"It's a service to our favored customers."

When I looked dubious Wystan said, "Ten percent discount to our favored customers. Regular book sales."

But mutely I shook my head *no*.

No thanks.

"Or an email address, then."

But I was feeling cautious. *No thanks!*

Wystan opened the door for me with a show of gallantry. I had to pass close by his extended arm, and I could smell his particular odor—book-dust, papery-dry-dust, long melancholy afternoons shading into night. Suddenly with a quizzical smile he asked me if I knew Harvey Selden?—and quickly I shook my head *no*.

"You remind me of Harvey. Around the eyes, I think. And the nose—you both have a kind of 'patrician' nose."

My heart beat strangely. Why I felt such alarm, I don't know. As if I were about to receive a profound and irrevocable revelation, and did not know if I was ready for it.

Wystan said, with a look of regret, "Harvey is the most remarkable person I've met. Not that I know Harvey well—I don't. Never did. He can read all kinds of crazy languages of 'antiquity.' He was translating something from the Bible, he thought would 'transform' the world. He used to come into the store two-three times a week when he'd first moved to Trenton in May. Bought lots of books—cheap paperbacks but great choices. He was a 'seminarian' he said—on 'sabbatical' for a term. But lately, last five weeks or so, I haven't seen him and I kind of miss him. I'd been saving out some special old books for him. Someone who'd met Harvey here in the store, who sometimes hangs out here, said the other day, really shook me up, that Harvey had died—just last week."

"Died! Of what?"

"In Trenton, it almost doesn't matter how. Death just *comes*."

"But—how?"

"That wasn't clear. A drug overdose, maybe. Or a drug dealer wanting the money Harvey owed him."

5.

Often when I returned home, the apartment was empty.

A look as of having been ravaged, ransacked.

Smells of tobacco smoke, or hashish. Distinctive yet inexplicable *smells*.

Slowly I would make my way into Harvey's bedroom, and then his bathroom—hoping I would not find his body collapsed on the floor.

And in the little nursery at the rear of the apartment—a patch of shadow beneath my desk-table made me start, and cry out in alarm.

"Oh!"—though I could see that it was nothing.

Thinking *It won't matter how. It just—comes.*

And who else lived in the quasi-renovated English Tudor at 11 Grindell?

Harvey knew none of his neighbors. They appeared to be, with the exception of an elderly white couple who lived below Harvey, on the first floor, a shifting population that sometimes included young children, mostly dark-skinned, with a scattering of "whites"—individuals who avoided my eye when we happened to meet in the vestibule, or on the stairs. In one of the third-floor apartments, a few days after I'd arrived to stay with Harvey, there was some sort of medical emergency: a loud siren, loud voices and footsteps on the stairs, a woman's uplifted frightened voice, shouted instructions and cries and Harvey forbidding me to open the door: "You don't want to know, Lydia. And I sure don't, either."

Beneath Harvey, on the first floor, lived an elderly white couple who seemed rarely to leave their apartment, surname *Baumgarten*. They were so quiet, even in the aftermath of noise and clamor in my brother's apartment, I worried for their well-being—"What if they've died, and no one knows? Shouldn't we check on them?"—and Harvey said, frowning, "No. That's a terrible idea."

Once, I did knock on the Baumgartens' door, 1B. After a very long time the door was opened a crack, and a single eye, lashless, naked, staring in suspicion, appeared at about the level of my chin.

Yes? What do you want?—a suspicious whispery voice inquired.

And I could not think how to reply—*Nothing! I want nothing from you only just—some evidence that you are—that you are not—that you are* alive.

But I could not utter such ridiculous words. I could not utter anything convincing or halfway reasonable stammering finally *Excuse me! I'm so sorry to interrupt you, I think I have the wrong address . . .*

The door shut, the door was bolted from within.

I never caught a glimpse of the Baumgartens again.

One of the assignments I'd brought to Trenton was a bound galley of a slender book titled *Cleansing Rituals: Mother, Infant, Taboo* which appeared to be a doctoral dissertation by a young assistant professor of anthropology at UC-Berkeley.

I felt that familiar thrill of rivalry! Envy.

Yet: I was determined to be utterly fair and judicious in my review. Where I wasn't qualified to criticize, I would not criticize. I would look for much to praise.

It was an honor, I'd thought, and a matter of some pride, that the prestigious *Journal of the Anthropology of Religion* had asked me to do a brief, five-hundred-word review of the book. It was not common for editors of such a peer-reviewed journal to assign reviews to academicians like myself who were so young, and lacking a Ph.D., and had not yet published books themselves. But the editors of the *Journal* had heard me present a paper at a conference at Columbia University in September and had sent me the galley to review, to my surprise. Yet more of a surprise was my thesis advisor Professor A.'s reaction: he had scarcely been impressed but rather sourly he'd warned me not to "squander" my energy in transient tasks, at this time in my career when completing a substantial dissertation was crucial.

I was disappointed, and hurt. It seemed to be a melancholy pattern in my life, I brought to others news of achievements which I would have thought might impress them, or cause them to feel pride for me; but the reaction was totally antipathetic. I could not *predict.*

So frequently the term *taboo* occurs in anthropological research, it would be helpful to know what *taboo* means.

But we can know only the *taboos* of others, which we can coolly deconstruct. Our own, private *taboos* are hidden to us as the contours of our own brains.

My subject was a number of linked ancient texts dealing with rituals of childbirth/motherhood. In these texts, there were no father-figures—no father-deities—only the pregnant female, the female-in-childbirth, the female and her infant, and female "spirits" ("demons"?).

The number of ancient manuscripts dealing with twins must have been hugely disproportionate to the number of twins born, which was a puzzle. In this culture twins were likely to be "sacred twins"—unless they were "demon twins." The obsessive subject prevailed across different cultures and eras and into the present day in Africa—much about the rituals was similar, yet, unaccountably, there were rituals that seemed to contradict the others.

Some twins were "sacred" and beloved. Some twins were "demonic" and were to be killed immediately at birth. In one text, the fullness of the moon seemed to be a relevant factor; in another, the nature of the delivery—whether it was exceedingly bloody, for instance. (If the mother died in childbirth, "sacred" twins were reared by the tribe; "demonic" twins were to be executed at once, and not buried with the mother.) Yet these issues were hedged with doubt and ambivalence and the effort of translating the relevant manuscripts was challenging, for there were words that, translated, might mean what they usually meant or their opposite. And there were key words that baffled translators. In such cases infanticide was not considered murder but "ritual cleansing." Professor A. had written extensively of the puzzles and paradoxes of the Eweian texts which dated from A.D. 700 yet retained older, ancient passages and single words that had become extinct by A.D. 700 so it was not clear what the author of the text meant by them. Professor A. had spent much of his mid-career on this paradoxical subject and had tried to explain to me where the more crucial problems lay. Basically, Professor A. was involved in a genteel feud with other translators and scholars for it was his belief that the texts had been inadequately translated—the (unclean) infants had not been murdered but in some literal way "cleansed." There was a Eweian term—*sRjAApuna*—that can be translated as "cleansing"— "eradicating"—"purifying"—(more rarely) "destroying." There were recipes for sacred ointments, baths, amulets to "purify"—or "protect"—the mother who had just given birth, who would have been, like all such mothers, then as now, extremely vulnerable to lethal infections; except these ancient people did not know about bacterial infections, only that mothers often died in childbirth, a time of terrible "uncleanliness." In all this, the taboo functioned mysteriously: some sort of (never-spoken) acknowledgment of the Great Mother, represented as a genial sort of demon with ornamental skulls around her neck.

Working on the Eweian texts, I sometimes felt that I understood the intent of the manuscript clearly, as if the author were not an ancient scribe—male, more likely than female—but a kindred soul; yet, the next day when I sat down to work, I felt that I did not understand at all, and that the arcane and forbidden vocabulary would never yield to my attempts to decode it.

I did know, from my conversations with Professor A., that Professor A. would not favor any text-translation that suggested that the ritual cleansings were ritual murders—ritual infanticide. I knew this, and hoped that I would have enough integrity to insist upon my own interpretation, eventually.

How I wished that I could work with Nyame manuscripts—the famous text of ancient times in which the "sacred trinity" is established: God the father, God the mother, and God the son. In all, to the Nyame people, who'd once lived in the general region of Zimbabwe, God was not a singular individual, not a master-monster, but a *family*.

(Too bad, there wasn't God the daughter, too. But this notion of a *family-God* seemed wonderful to me, enviable.)

Once, I'd said to Professor A., "Why is so much of primitive life ritual? What *is* ritual?" and Professor A. said, as if he'd answered this question many times in his career, "Ritual eliminates chance. The originality and errors of chance. Ritual is repetition. Repetition becomes 'sacred.' Our ancestors know, as we know, that we can't trust 'chance.' We must have reasons for what we do, even if they are unreasonable."

I knew that I had misspoken: I should not have used the expression *primitive*.

But when I tried to apologize for this politically incorrect, anachronistic term, Professor A. laughed as if conspiratorially saying, "Well, let's be frank, Lydia. There are 'primitive peoples' even today—'aboriginals.' Much of the world—the African continent, surely—except for South Africa—is primitive. Witch doctors drilling holes in people's skulls to release demons. Worse than the Roman Catholic exorcism—though that's 'primitive' enough. And when the patient dies, it's the demon who killed him, not the witch doctor."

Hesitantly I said, "'Infanticide'—it's the most powerful taboo. But animals commit it, we know—in the service of evolution. I mean, an animal mother will kill the 'runt of the litter' or let him die—or be eaten by his siblings—because she can't care for him, and too much of her strength will be squandered in a lost cause." I had not meant to say *squandered* but it was too late to retract it.

Professor A. stared at me in surprise. Now truly I had misspoken.

Darwinian evolutionary theory was not so very welcome in Professor A.'s field, for its simple, much-reiterated theorems about the instinct for survival at all costs and the instinct to reproduce the species trumped more complex scholarly speculations of a kind that required a lifetime to master. What if infanticide wasn't a ritual taboo but—just a commonplace in animal and human life? Arcane texts, beautiful extinct languages, decades of struggle to define single words and phrases—what did precision of translation matter, if each ritual had as its primary concern the evolutionary advantage of the individual, and through the individual, the species?

Coldly Professor A. said, "I think, Lydia—that is your name, isn't it: Lydia?—it will be wisest for you to stay very close to your texts. Word by word, line by line, passage by passage—you are walking a tightrope over an abyss, as a responsible translator. All speculation—the lifeblood of other sciences—is abhorrent to the anthropologist, who deals in *facts*."

You will not disobey me. You are the captive daughter.

In Grindell Park, at my makeshift desk, I puzzled over the Eweian text as if I'd never seen it before. Originally I'd been thrilled by the challenge—if my translation was a good one, and Professor A. approved it, very likely it would be published in a prestigious journal; such a publication would have an immeasurable effect upon my young career. Professor A. had virtually handed me this gift—yet now, irresponsibly, I had a fantasy of ripping it into pieces—that is, the photocopied text; but what good would that do? All that Professor A. had entrusted to me was a sixteen-page photocopy of the "sacred" text miraculously preserved from antiquity and now kept under lock and key in the University library's hallowed special collection.

I thought *Individuals die, life endures. A copy of a text is destroyed but another takes its place—just like us.*

6.

Voices inside. Unmistakable.

And when I turned the doorknob, the door was locked.

"Harvey? It's—me . . ."

The voices continued, punctuated by laughter. A sharp staccato series of barks—Dargo?

". . . it's Lydia, will you let me inside?"

I knocked on the door. Knocked, banged my fist. Manic dog-barking ensued. I thought *I have the right, he can't keep me out. I live here too, now.*

More soberly I thought *If the door is opened, the pit bull will rush at me. No one will stop him.*

Still I waited in the hall. I pressed my ear against the door. I thought I heard Harvey's voice—muffled, indistinct. I was sure that I heard Leander's voice, and another male voice.

Possibly, a female voice. Maralena?

I was holding bags of groceries in both my arms, which I'd purchased not at Pinneo's Market but several miles north in a Trenton suburb, at a ShopRite. In this store there was "fresh" produce, better quality food overall, and, unexpectedly, the price of my purchases was slightly less than it would have been at the corner market on Camden Avenue.

I knocked another time. The dog's barking was hysterical now. They must have known who was at the door, who was desperate to be admitted, but no one opened the door, no one spoke to me.

I retreated to my car. Locked the groceries in the trunk and walked over to the little library to wait there, abashed and humbled, until closing time.

He has betrayed me, my brother. It is strangers he loves.

Another time when I was in my study working on the Eweian translation Harvey came to the doorway to inform me that he was shutting my door and that under no circumstances was I to open it—"Someone is coming here. If he sees you he'll be suspicious. If he's suspicious there could be trouble. There could be danger. Not only to me but to you."

"Danger? What—"

"No time to quibble. Just don't open this door."

"But—who is coming? What's happening?"

"God damn, Lydia, I've warned you—just don't open this door."

Harvey's eyes looked as if they were shadowed in grime. His smile had become gap-toothed. Overnight, in some bizarre episode of which I knew nothing, he seemed to have lost one of his lower front teeth. Like a deranged Hallowe'en pumpkin my brother grinned, or grimaced; his facial features were so agitated and twitchy, I couldn't distinguish a grin from a grimace.

"Stay inside. It will be fine. He'll arrive, and he'll depart. It will go well. *Just don't open the door and show your face.*"

Harvey shut the door. I heard him dragging something, a heavy piece of furniture, to buttress against it, to prevent my opening it.

Immediately I went to the door, and tried the knob. I could not budge the door open, I was trapped.

Soon there came a sound of someone arriving at the apartment: a man's voice. Not a voice I recognized. And a second voice, also a man's, and unrecognizable.

Harvey's voice was a murmur, indecipherable.

Whatever the transaction was, it did not take more than fifteen minutes. By which time in my desperation I had worked out a plan. *If they kill Harvey, I will not be trapped here. I can scream out the window. I can climb out the window onto the roof. I will not die here. Not with Harvey.*

Seven weeks, living with Harvey. As our parents had bade me.

It was true, I now shopped for my brother. I prepared meals for my brother which sometimes he ate, or partially ate. There was an unexpected pleasure in this—the simplicity of providing meals for another. To prepare something that would give pleasure to another *in the next several minutes*. For otherwise, my connection to the world was purely abstract.

Rarely did I think now of Professor A. Or of my room in Newcomb Hall where the residence advisor must have thought I'd quit graduate school without notifying anyone.

Each morning I vowed to re-establish my residence at the University, if only through a telephone call or email. For I very much feared that my fellowship installments would be terminated.

By each evening, I'd forgotten.

Harvey seemed less resentful of me now. He seemed to have accepted it, I'd moved into his life.

His secret life, I'd never entirely penetrated. Though I had ideas of what this secret life was—obviously.

More frequently Harvey began to confide in me. When the shadow-grime was gone from his eyes, and his eyes were relatively clear. When his voice wasn't raddled with phlegm but relatively clear. And the space where his tooth was missing wasn't so visible.

He hadn't given up the seminary, he insisted. He was on a kind of—sabbatical.

Nor had he given up his scholarly project. If I heard him muttering in his room, it was Aramaic he was speaking—to himself.

"Obviously, a scholar who knows six languages is more equipped than one who knows only three or four. A scholar who knows sixteen languages is more equipped than one who knows only six. There's no place for specialists who immerse themselves in a single culture now—that's not the way things are done today."

He couldn't proceed, Harvey said, without a more complete knowledge of Sanskrit than he had. He'd never learned ancient Macedonian, and knew just the rudiments of Mycenaean Greek.

His voice quavered. I saw the madness shimmering before him like a mirage—you will never know enough languages, you will never know enough of anything. You are broken, defeated. You must throw your life away to avoid humiliation.

Problem was, Harvey continued, his brain had finally cracked like a patch of arid earth. You've seen cracks in the earth, so Harvey described his cracked brain.

This had happened, this cracking, about eighteen months before. He'd tried to keep going for as long as he could with his cracked brain but finally even his prescribed medications had failed him. He'd had to remove himself to Trenton where there were "some people" he'd come to know—"To save my life."

Only a week before I'd arrived Harvey had collapsed on the street, been brought by ambulance to the local ER where it was discovered that he was "severely dehydrated," and so he was hospitalized, and IV fluids dripped into his veins to prevent renal failure. On the third day of his hospitalization he'd detached the IV line from the crook of his arm and managed to slip out of the hospital and find his way back to Grindell Park.

Are you a drug addict?—I could not bring myself to ask. *Are you a junkie?*

He needed to have professional help, I told him. If he'd allow me, I could assist him.

"Help? Too late."

"A clinic, rehab—"

"Rehab? Too late."

Harvey sneered, laughing. His eyes, which I'd believed to be clear and alert, seemed to be occluding over.

Daringly I said, "What exactly is—what *is it*, Harvey? I wish you'd tell me."

"Nothing to tell except I've been *rehabilitated*. What you see before you is *rehabilitation.*"

The air in Harvey's apartment was so close and stale, I had to stagger out, outside. In my car parked at the curb I sat for a while dazed and stunned until several of the gangsta boys in Grindell Park drifted around the car, tapped at the windows, grinned and laughed at me mouthing words—(obscenities?)—my averted eyes could not decipher.

Eventually, they drifted away. As dusk neared, their customers began to arrive. Quite possibly, I was under Leander's protection. They would know this. They would honor this. I was one of Leander's white girls, safe in his protection.

Here was Harvey's secret, revealed at last: he was writing poetry.

"Poetry? *You?*"

Chiseling poetry, it felt like. Digging in stone with his fingernails.

(Saying this, Harvey lifted his hands to stare at his ragged broken nails. The stump of his smallest finger, right hand.)

I did not know what to say in reply to Harvey's sudden pronouncement. I associated poetry-writing with a brave and reckless futility beyond that of scholarly research into extinct languages and could not imagine taking up such a futility, of my own volition.

Surely poetry-writing was a curse. Particularly in America where the poetry of street-speech, the poetry of popular culture, and the poetry of finance were supreme.

"Can I see some of your poems, Harvey? Please."

It was one of our dinnertimes. When Harvey consented to eat, or partially eat, one of the meals I prepared for him. Many of our dinners were pasta, with (canned) tomato sauce to which

I'd added onions, fresh tomatoes, and spices—oregano, basil, red pepper. Another of our meals was scrambled eggs, or an approximation of an omelet into which I'd stirred fried onions, red peppers, mushrooms. If Harvey was in an Up Mood he would eat, hungrily. (For poor Harvey was wasting away, his hands big-knuckled as the skin shrank and tightened over the knobby bones.) In an Up Mood, he might even praise me which suffused my heart like a surge of warm blood—how yearning I was, to be praised, therefore loved! (Though Harvey might also muddle my name, confusing "Lydia" with another of our sisters, to whom he'd been closer when we were growing up.)

In a Down Mood, Harvey could not eat. And if he tried to eat, he became nauseated and began to gag. (And worse.) In a Down Mood Harvey was too restless to sit still for long but paced about the apartment's airless rooms muttering to himself—Aramaic? (It might as well have been Sanskrit or Mycenaean Greek for all that I knew.) Compulsively he went to the window to peer out, and down at the street; he went to the door, to open it and peer out into the hall; each time his cell phone rang, he leapt to answer it; each time there was a noise out in the street, or on the stairs, he twitched and jumped as if he were being exquisitely tortured.

If a call came on Harvey's cell, he spoke in a lowered voice so that I couldn't hear. Shortly afterward he would leave the apartment not to return until late that evening and if I tried to call his cell, which he'd taken with him, my call went directly to voice mail leaving me in a void.

But it was in one of Harvey's Up Moods that he told me about writing poetry—his "decision" to become a poet.

At dinner he'd had two or three glasses of wine with our spicy spaghetti sauce and pasta. He was led to confide in me: "Poetry is not statement but *sound*. Poetry is *music*."

And: "A poet is one who communicates to the heart, through *sound*."

I asked Harvey to read me one or two of his poems but he seemed shy suddenly. Or whatever Harvey was when he retreated inside his head—stubborn, sulky.

"You wouldn't understand. You're an 'intellectual.'"

I wanted to protest *You're an intellectual! I am just an imitation.*

"None of my poems are finished. I have hundreds of fragments —shimmering and transient as flies' wings. Poetry is our revenge against the stupidity of society. Poetry is beautiful but can hurt, like whirring blades."

I had not heard Harvey speak so passionately for years. Once, he'd spoken in such a tone about God.

In a voice carefully controlled so that no emotion was revealed Harvey recited: "'Dawn-dusk-dew. Even-ing. Lunar scape. Rhomboidal radiance.'" He waited, breathing audibly. It was as if my very private brother had torn open his shirt to reveal his naked chest, his beating heart, to me.

I felt a wild impulse to laugh. *Rhomboidal radiance!* It would be futile to ask what this could possibly mean, for of course, as Harvey would say, poetry does not *mean*.

Harvey said, "It's the dreamy vowels of 'dawn-dusk-dew' that are seductive. And the beautiful word which I've broken into twin spondees—'even-ing.' Note the drawn-out sound of 'lunar' and the harsher nasal sound of the '*a*' of 'scape.'"

I told Harvey that it was very—interesting.

"A poetry of sheer *sound*. For the inner ear—the *soul*."

Harvey paused, shutting his eyes. A noise in the near distance, as of a firecracker exploding, or gunfire, did not distract him. "'Sleek-sleet-sky-shattering.'"

"Very—striking."

"'Tight fists of shit.'"

Seeing my startled reaction Harvey laughed, pleased.

"Actually, that's my single complete poem, a haiku. The title explains all—'Self-Portrait America 2012'—'Tight fists of shit.'"

This "haiku" was stunning to me. The ferocity with which Harvey recited it suggested a meaning far deeper than the merely musical.

"It's ingenious, Harvey. Three spondees, isn't it?"

"Essentially, yes. 'Tight fists' and 'shit' are spondees—'of' is lightly stressed. If read properly, the poem embodies its (unintended) meaning: 'Tight fists of shit.' You will note the strong '*i*' repetition."

Harvey opened his eyes wide now, and was staring rudely at me. As if he'd detected something forced and fraudulent beneath my schoolgirl enthusiasm.

"Do you have any other poems? I'd like to—"

"Not that you'd like, I think."

Harvey's face shut up tight. A few seconds later, as if the caller had been purposefully waiting, his cell phone rang and he staggered off to answer it, in the other room.

Then, there were interrupted mealtimes.

Loud knocking at the door, and it was Leander, Tin, and Maralena.

Harvey hurried to let them in. Harvey offered them wine, ordering me in a lowered voice to wash our glass tumblers.

"Lydia was just making dinner. Will you stay? Eat with us?"

Leander grinned and shrugged, as if he were doing us a favor. Tin frowned, staring down at the floor; he seemed deeply moved. Festive Maralena said, "Ohhh thank you, Har-vey! We would sure love that."

Maralena insisted upon helping me at the stove. Boiling pasta, checking to see if it was *al dente* before dumping it into the colander. In the cramped kitchen area Maralena laughed and gossiped with me as if we were old friends, or sisters. Several times she nudged against me as if accidentally, like a big upright purring cat.

The men sat at the table, drinking. But they drank red wine as if it were beer, or a soft drink. Leander's wild dreadlocks tumbled down his narrow muscled back and the Maori tattoo on his face glared whitely against his purplish-dark skin. Tin, flat-faced, small-eyed, vaguely Asian, was so solid-fleshed, the chair he sat in creaked and wobbled. Leander teased, "You fat-ass! Watch you'self you gon break these people's nice chair." It was part of Leander's humor, the chair in which Tin was sitting was secondhand and the vinyl seat soiled and certainly not *nice.*

Tin muttered what sounded like *Fuck you.* His flat face darkened with blood.

Harvey seemed dazed by our visitors, whose presence transformed the bleak setting. Leander was swaggering and charismatic as a rap star, Maralena gorgeous as the singer whose name I didn't know how to pronounce—*Beyoncé.* Even Tin, homely, strangely self-effacing, with a small mouth like a vise, exerted a curious sort of attraction. Beside these *so physical* individuals Harvey and I felt to ourselves like white-skinned wraiths.

And there was Maralena carrying plates of steaming-hot food to the table, slyly nudging her thigh against Harvey's arm.

Maralena wore gold lamé pants so tight they might have been poured molten onto her shapely buttocks, belly and legs. And, on her shapely torso, a black jersey tank top. When she'd arrived at the door she'd been wearing a *faux*-fox jacket over these clothes and on her head her shoulder-length cornrowed hair quivered like slithery little snakes.

Though I was nervous in the presence of our unexpected guests it was exciting to me to be feeding them. And my brother Harvey, who was my entire family now. Again I felt the happiness of bringing pleasure to others in an immediate and observable way.

Leander, Tin, and Maralena ate hungrily. At the ShopRite I'd bought a loaf of French bread which they broke into large pieces, shoved into the spaghetti sauce, and devoured.

"Real good, Lyd'ja!"

"Re-al good, girl."

Maralena seemed just slightly surprised, my cooking was so tasty.

They ate, and they drank. In a daze of happiness Harvey filled their tumblers with red wine. Flat-faced Tin never spoke but only grunted, moving his jaws like a masticating insect.

After dinner, Maralena helped me clear away the plates, rinse and wash them by hand. "You a true sister to you' brother, Lyd'ja. L'nd'r be takin note of that."

What Maralena meant, I had no idea. Her exotic eyes were fixed on me, I found it difficult to breathe.

And Maralena's special fragrance, that wafted from her hair and from the dip of her black jersey tank top revealing a shadowy crevice between her breasts.

"Thing is, girl, you' brother in some deep shit-hole with L'nd'r. Feedin him some nice meal like this is a good thing. L'nd'r got *heart,* no matter what his enemies say of him he be *stone cold killer.*"

Maralena had spoken just loudly enough so that Leander could overhear this remark if he wished. He'd been leaning back in his chair and now let the legs slam against the floor, hard. "Shut you' mouth, 'Lena, or somebody shut it for you. You read me?"

Maralena giggled, shivering. To me she said, "That boy just talkin. He ain't gon touch any blood-kin of his, he know what that bring on his head."

Leander sneered, "You sure of that, girl?"

Boldly Maralena said, "Dint I just say I *was*?"

Now the table was cleared, Leander suggested that they play poker—just him, Tin, and Harvey.

Leander flourished a pack of cards. Showily shuffling them like a professional player.

I saw that Harvey wanted to say *yes*. But that Harvey knew he should say *no*.

Harvey tugged at his mutilated ear, which was slow to heal and often itched.

"You, Tin? You in, eh?"

Tin nodded impassively.

"Har-vey, my man?"

Harvey moved his head, numbly. A foolish smile transforming Harvey's stubbled face.

Maralena said to me, "They be practicin for 'Lantic City, where they gon get their asses kicked at poker." She giggled, running her fingers through her cousin's greased plaits in a way that seemed daring to me, provocative. Leander slapped at her hand. Maralena laughed and stepped away from Leander who was glaring at her, not smiling. Just slightly shaken—(I think this was so)—Maralena slid her arm around my waist, tight. "My girl friend Lyd'ja and me gon hang out in Lyd'ja's room listenin to some mad cool music. You boys be nice to you' host now, you hear me?"

Maralena walked me out of the living room and in the direction of the bedroom. It seemed strange to me, Maralena seemed to know her way around my brother's apartment. Behind us I heard Harvey's slow voice: "What kind of—stakes? Are we playing for money? The problem is, Leander—I don't have much cash right on hand, which you might know."

"Shit man, sure I know. This be some friendly way Tin an me, we gon give you the opportunity to win big, climb up out of you' deep hole. See?"

Maralena led me forcibly away. Though it didn't feel *forcible* since I didn't try to resist.

Next day, Harvey lay comatose in his bed until noon.

He'd lost—oh Christ!—money to the boys.

How much, I asked.

Too much, Harvey said.

How much, please tell me.

Harvey flung his arm over his face, shivering and shuddering. He seemed about to speak further to me but then I heard his shallow erratic breathing, indicating that he'd fallen back to sleep.

All that I knew was that the three men had been playing poker and drinking and (just possibly) smoking hashish after Maralena had gone home at midnight and I'd lain on my bed partially undressed, and fell asleep to voices laughing and cursing in the other room.

It is family life almost.

They would not hurt family—would they?

The situation seemed grave to me. Soon, Leander would come by to collect.

More than a finger-stub. More than a part of an ear.

There was thirteen hundred dollars in my bank account. I would write a check for half this amount, to give to Harvey—if Harvey would promise me he wouldn't spend it on something else but give it to Leander.

"Of course," Harvey said eagerly.

"But—you promise? You will give it to Leander?"

Harvey insisted, yes.

I didn't trust Harvey. But I didn't think that I had any choice in the matter.

In my bedroom, which was also my study, we'd listened to music from Maralena's iPhone. Heated dance music it sounded to me, a Latin beat, rap from the islands Maralena said, the DR where she'd been born and from which she'd been brought—by her mother—at the age of five. Much of what Maralena confided in me I didn't understand, mesmerized by her rich warm musical voice and by her rich warm fragrant skin, the Maralena eyes, the Maralena nose, the Maralena mouth tasting of wine kissing me, lifting her wineglass to my mouth, urging me to drink, red wine that was nutty-sweet, a dark-nutty-sweetness that numbed the interior of my mouth and the interior of my skull as Maralena kissed my forehead, my nose, my mouth and Maralena kissed the ticklish inside of my neck so that I squirmed breathless and helpless and I was lying on the sofa that Harvey and I had dragged into the room which served now as my bed, badly stained and sagging sofa of a kind you'd see abandoned behind a Dumpster, but over this I'd draped a blanket so you couldn't see the stains and wear-and-tear of decades and Maralena was sharp-voiced suddenly wanting to keep me from falling asleep, shaking my shoulders and her talon fingernails sinking into my skin—"You, girl! Lyd-ja! Wake up!"—her voice urgent, alarmed; so that I thought *She has fed me something. Some drug* but the thought was a frail straw not nearly substantial enough to jolt me into wakefulness.

And there came, later, maybe only a few minutes later, or in the middle of the night, which is not a true "night" in Trenton but a glowering-dark riddled with light like wormholes, and punctuated with sharp percussive noises like the *snap!* of the soul as it breaks from the writhing body, the boy with the Maori mask-face, the boy with the headdress of greased and pungent-smelling dreadlocks tumbling down his muscled back, and Maralena pushed at him, and he pushed at Maralena, *Noooo* she was pleading, or maybe she was laughing-pleading, for you don't say *Noooo* to Leander, not a serious *Noooo* and there came a creaking of the sofa springs, and Leander's rough fingers scrambling down my body like a ravenous rat, and between my legs these fingers were poking, between my helpless legs these hard probing fingers defined themselves grabbing, pinching, squeezing, poking-into; and feebly I tried to detach myself, muttering in my sleep in an extinct language I tried to protest, and Leander grunted swinging his legs onto the sofa, prying my legs apart, and Maralena was faint now at the door or already outside the door calling back over her shoulder *Damn ol' swine, that girl too white for you—you break her li'l white neck asshole you gon regret it.*

In the morning my neck ached—my spine, the small of my back, the insides of my thighs, between my legs which was chafed and ravaged as with the incisors of a devouring rat—but my neck was not broken and my memory dim and retreating and therefore consoling. *You can't remember, whatever did or did not happen is on the far side of a chasm of memory which you cannot cross.* Soon then seeking out Harvey whose shallow breathing and pallid skin worried me, at first glimpse my brother appeared to be scarcely alive as if flung across his rumpled bed where his poker-friends had left him and I'd managed to wake him out of that stuporous suffocating sleep and he'd cursed me wanting badly to remain in that sleep and lamenting oh Christ!—first memory that came to him, he'd lost more money; and I asked, How much, how much money did you lose to them and he said, Too much. And then he said, Don't ask, you don't want to know.

7.

He'd become shorter. Losing height. In the crook of his arm was a deep gash, slowly healing. He claimed it was from the IV line the ER nurses had put into his arm, that had become infected.

On a battered calendar of Harvey's I saw a pattern of red *x*'s. Less frequently, blue *x*'s.

I asked him what the red *x*'s meant and Harvey shrugged. None of my concern.

I asked him what the blue *x*'s meant and Harvey said, Rehab.

But the blue *x*'s were only scattered through a month. The red *x*'s were several times a week.

Getting high?—red had to mean an Up Mood.

Blue?—the Down Mood.

I told Harvey, please let me drive you to the rehab clinic. You must have a schedule of treatment there, you can't afford to miss.

(Was Harvey trying to cure himself of his drug addiction? Or had Harvey some other, medical condition, for which he was being treated? I'd gathered from careless remarks he'd made that he had infusions at the clinic—his white blood count was "low" and he was anemic.)

I knew to urge my brother to drink water. Several glasses of water a day.

"There's a danger of dehydration. You don't eat, drink, sleep, take care of yourself properly."

" 'De-hy-dra-tion.' "

Harvey contemplated the word as if tasting it on his tongue. But the taste didn't interest him.

"Harvey, you could die."

" 'Harvey, you could die.' " Harvey considered this phrase, dubiously. "It doesn't scan. It doesn't fly. Though the vowels exude a kind of dull-anxious concern. A kind of *mock concern.* Not that this fictitious 'Harvey' will die but merely *could die.* Which is a fact for all who live—*could die.*"

Harvey seemed to be paying only a peripheral attention to me, absently caressing his mutilated ear that flamed when so touched.

"'How scale walls of Hades'—this came to me last night. In the night. Note the short '*a*' sound. Vowels are a sort of string upon which words are strung. I think so. I think this is my discovery, but it may perish with me." Harvey laughed, scratching the flaming ear.

It was late morning. I saw that Harvey would not speak to me in any serious way. Another day lost to us. Unless I worked on the Eweian translation in which, in fact, I had lost faith. Yet working diligently and even obsessively *without faith* did not seem to me a terrible fate, when the alternative was yet more terrible.

In the apartment there were strange languidly wafting odors. Each day, new odors emerged of faint decay, rot. I'd thought it was the ancient refrigerator but even after I'd cleaned and scrubbed the interior, the smells remained. When I was gone from the apartment, to work in the little library for instance, and returned, the odors were always slightly different, as if the air had been agitated in my absence. Especially if I was away for some time. The apartment might show signs of visitors—rearranged chairs, boxes of books shoved from one place to another. And Harvey sprawled on a small sofa in the living room, notebook on his knee like one who has made a refuge for himself in the midst of great chaos: earthquake, flood.

At Harvey's nose, a perpetual glisten of moisture.

He is a junkie. You know of course. A junkie has no shame.

In a bemused voice Harvey said, as if thinking aloud: "Montaigne discovered at the age of thirty-eight that death is light and airy—he'd been thrown from his horse, trampled. He experienced no 'other world'—no God, no Savior. He'd been Catholic of course—everyone was Catholic at that time and in that place, in sixteenth-century France. Montaigne saw that life is the long haul. Dying is the easy way."

"And how did Montaigne know this?" I asked, exasperated. "Had he died, and returned to write about the experience?"

"He almost died. It was *near*-death. His 'soul' slipped from his body, according to his account. For some time, he floated outside his broken body."

"We all do," I said. "It's called dreaming."

"Lyd'ja! You gon drive us to 'Lantic City, yes?"

Somehow it was—*yes*.

Couldn't say *no* to Maralena. Basking in Maralena's hectic warmth and when Maralena spoke of Lyd'ja as *my girl friend* I felt such happiness, no poetry could begin to express.

With Maralena was her *girl friend* Salaman. And another *girl friend* Mercedes.

It was upsetting to me, when Maralena came to our apartment with her cousin Leander. Made me sick with jealousy when Maralena joked with flat-faced Tin.

And sometimes, I had reason to think that Maralena and girl friends of hers came into the apartment with other men, individuals whose faces were becoming almost familiar to me, though I had no idea of their names or who they were—shadowy figures at the periphery of my brother's life. It wasn't clear to me whether Harvey was being exploited by these individuals or whether in some mysterious way Harvey was exploiting them.

Those nights when Harvey hastily shoved me into the back room—"For your own safety, Lydia."

Somehow it happened, I was to drive Maralena, Salaman, and Mercedes to Atlantic City. Leaving in the early afternoon from Trenton and returning that night late.

Maralena, Salaman, Mercedes—these were dazzling young women with faces of the kind you see on billboards beckoning you to the casinos of Atlantic City.

I felt privileged to be driving them. To be their white-skinned *girl friend*.

Harvey smiled a pinched smile. Harvey might've been jealous.

Saying, meanly, "They will bleed you dry, little sister. Be forewarned."

I didn't think so. Maralena was my *girl friend*.

Hadn't Maralena given me her cell phone number with the admonition to call her *any time day, night* if I needed help.

Let myself be cajoled into driving Maralena and her friends to Atlantic City and to "lending" them money—most of what remained of what I'd withdrawn from my University account.

Of the Atlantic City casino-hotels—among them Trump Taj Mahal, Bally's, Harrah's, Tropicana, Borgata—it was the *faux*-luxurious Borgata my friends preferred; Showboat and Rio they scorned as "low-roller" casinos—"For old folks, that come in buses. And some in wheelchairs, in buses."

We started off at the slots. Here was low-stakes gambling, a kind of bargain-basement gambling that carried with it nonetheless a certain amount of drama and suspense. At least for those who expected they might win.

Pulling a lever to start into motion cartoon-fruit symbols spinning past my face seemed to me a gesture of such extreme futility, there was a childish abandon to it. Or maybe it was just the nearness of Maralena, Salaman, Mercedes who were dressed like giant tropical birds in tight-fitting sparkly clothes, high heels, dark-lace stockings. Maralena had silver piercings in her ears and left eyebrow; Salaman had dark-red-streaked hair and piercings in her face and elsewhere, she hinted, inside her clothes; Mercedes, the youngest of the three, had both piercings and tattoos, visible and hidden, and the loudest shrieking parrot-laugh. Mercedes teetered in gold-gleaming high-heeled boots to the knee; she had to show her ID to get into the casino, a fake ID (so I gathered) but the bored security guard, charmed by the girls, didn't investigate closely.

Within minutes at the slots I'd lost thirty-six dollars' worth of tokens. Hardly a surprise!

I imagined Professor A. regarding me with stern disgusted eyes.

Lydia?—is that your name?

When someone won at slots—(which was fairly frequent, when the win wasn't a *big win*)—the machine lighted up giddily and music erupted in mock-hysterical celebration as, like a sudden spasm of vomiting, tokens flooded out of the mouth of the machine to be caught by the lucky winner in a cardboard container.

The idea was to arouse envious attention on the floor. To attract others to play the slots, imagining that they might *win big*.

My festive companions moved from machine to machine trying their luck. No skill was involved—just brainless luck. Of the three, Salaman actually came out eighteen dollars ahead.

"Girl, you gon *win big* tonight. This be a good prem'ition!"

On the drive from Trenton Maralena and her friends had spoken excitedly of a blackjack dealer whom they knew from Trenton, and it was this Jorge whom the girls sought amid the blackjack players. But no one seemed to have heard of Jorge— "Maybe he not workin tonight, that'd be shitty but you got to figure the man have to take some time off, yes?"—so Maralena reasoned. Much of the time Maralena was in the habit of addressing her girl friends with her back to me, as if she'd forgotten my presence. Their exchanges were high-pitched and bird-like and barely audible to me like exclamations in a foreign language amid the noise of the casino.

Why was I here! Why, with these glamorous young women whose toffee-colored skin glowed in the casino's delirious lights, drawing strangers' eyes irresistibly—why *me*?

Harvey had smiled pityingly at me when I'd left the apartment in my sole dress-up clothes—black nylon stretch-band slacks, cherry-colored velour top, black ballerina slippers. While I was driving on the Garden State Parkway to Atlantic City Maralena had tried playfully to "tease out" my hair with a comb, a pick, and hair spray, but the result was more of fright than of glamour.

"She real pretty," the girls said of me, to one another, as if I were not present, or couldn't be expected to understand their speech, "only the girl got *smile* more, show she *hot.*"

If Professor A. could see me now, with my *girl friends* in Atlantic City! I felt a deep flush of shame and incredulity at the thought.

(Professor A. had recently sent me an email, which I had not yet opened, still less answered. The director of the Newcomb Fellowship program had sent me several emails, which I had not yet opened. And there was some difficulty with the bank in the University town in which my fellowship installments were supposed to be deposited . . . All of these matters hovered in the distance like casino lights glittering and winking in the stark New Jersey night. Shut your eyes, such lights disappear.)

Gorgeous Maralena, Salaman, Mercedes were part of a small hectic crowd around a blackjack table. Was this a "hot" table? Were players winning here? The dealer wasn't Jorge it seemed but his dark-gleaming eyes slid onto Maralena, Salaman, Mercedes with a certain zestful recognition. He was a light-skinned Hispanic with a thin mustache, tight stylish clothes and a look of sly bemusement. A robot programmed for blackjack, the mechanical motions of a card game of stunning and lethal simplicity. His hands shuffled cards, his hands doled out cards, his hands swept up and retrieved cards and in the interstices of such motions your fate was determined: win, lose.

The girls were so fervent, so hopeful. Of course, they'd been drinking. Their drinks were festive and tropical as their clothing and hair. Not for their white-skinned *girl friend* Lyd'ja to warn them *The house always wins. That is the point of casino gambling.*

They'd have liked me less, if I spoiled their excitement with such warnings. Maralena would not swoop upon such a dour boring person and wetly kiss the corner of her mouth.

Within minutes, however, the girls had lost money at black-jack. Precious five-dollar tokens, swept away by the Hispanic dealer with the thin mustache. There had been the expectation— (maybe I'd felt this too)—at least, the childish hope—that being exceptionally pretty "sexy" girls with an obvious if unac-knowledged rapport with the blackjack dealer, that they would have a better chance of winning than more ordinary players of whom most were middle-aged white men with raddled jowls.

There had to be some special reward in Atlantic City, if not elsewhere, for looking like Maralena, Salaman, Mercedes.

"You play with us, Lyd'ja! C'mon, girl! We got to get back what we lost, can't go home broke!"—so they plucked at my sleeves.

"I don't think so," I said faltering, "blackjack isn't my—game," but they laughed at me, not altogether pleasantly I thought but as you'd laugh at an exasperating relative slowing you down by dragging a paralyzed leg, or a blundering blind relative. "We gon pay you back, Lyd-ja—long before we headin home. But you got to *help.*"

So I stood with them at the blackjack table. I was a hesitant player, destined to lose. At least at the slot machine my failure had been less conspicuous. Blackjack was an exhibitionist's game—you had to expect to win, or your instinct was to stand mute, and withdraw your tokens. To lose a bet *publicly*—this was hard.

But we lost. And we lost again.

"Fuck!"—Maralena's voice was not so musical now but New Jersey nasal and flat.

When we drifted from the blackjack table at which we'd lost, the blackjack dealer didn't so much as glance after us. Two row-dily inebriated couples pushed in eager to take our places.

Abruptly then we left the classy Borgata, which my companions bad-mouthed as a *stuck-up shitty place.* They'd bypassed craps, roulette, baccarat—these games intimidated them. Even blackjack took too much thinking. My companions thought of gambling as an opportunity to *win.*

The remainder of the Friday evening we spent at Trump Taj Mahal on the Boardwalk. Here, amid a sleazier sort of glamour, the girls seemed to feel more comfortable. The crowd was younger, less well dressed, with less money to spend; louder, brasher, more conspicuous drinkers. Despite its prime location on the Boardwalk, the Trump Taj Mahal was visibly run-down. (The famous Boardwalk itself was run-down, too. Homeless men were camping on benches and in doorways trying to shield themselves from the chill wind off the Atlantic Ocean; some of them looking so still, stiff and cold, wound in filthy blankets like mummies, Mercedes was moved to giggle nervously—*Them ain't corpses are they?*) But inside the garishly lit casino roaming men were attracted to the girls, bought them drinks and "bankrolled" them so that they could continue gambling.

This was the purpose of coming to Atlantic City, I realized. They'd made the trip before. They'd "gambled" here before. The prizes of the evening had to do with free money, so to speak, plucked by the girls like overripe fruit on a tree.

I did not mind being sidelined, watching. Like a chaperon, though I wasn't much older than my friends. Out of my black handbag which was nothing like the small glittery evening bags the girls were carrying I drew a half-dozen pages of the Eweian manuscript printout to read, or try to read, despite the dim lighting that made everything seem undersea.

Infanticide. Ritual cleansing. Not an act against the infant but an act of desperate self-survival. Involuntary, instinctive.

I thought this must be so. In a long-ago era before God entered time with His strictures of human moral behavior.

Yet, there were other aspects of the text in which the author's meaning was less clear. I was beginning to see that the ancient text contained another, secret text inside it. The surface text was just a patina, the truth lay beneath.

"Girl, put that shit away—it Friday night in 'Lantic City not some crappy ol' schoolroom."

Maralena and Salaman caught me squinting at the manuscript pages and slapped them out of my hand.

As the hours passed, the crowd in the casino increased. Roaming men appeared to be circling us like rogue-male animals. Some of them offered to buy us drinks, dinner. What principle my companions had for coldly dismissing such invitations, or warmly accepting them, I could not determine for all the men looked about equally attractive, or unattractive, to me.

Yet: how happy I was! Not knowing where I was.

The alcohol had gone to my head. I didn't know what one of the men had bought me—vodka? I heard myself laughing gaily.

"Are you these girls'—*teacher*? But what're you doing here, 'Lantic City on a Friday night?"

In the Taj my friends returned to blackjack. It was 10:20 P.M. Separated from them by other players, I could only see their backs—the backs of their heads. I felt a thrill of panic—I would lose them, they would be lost to me. Was I not responsible for them, driving them to Atlantic City in my car? For each girl had now a male companion, to buy her drinks and lend her precious tokens. I wondered what Leander would think of his sexy cousin's behavior. I wanted to think that Leander would disapprove, and sic Dargo on any predatory male.

I wasn't jealous. (I don't think so.) I wasn't envious. But maybe I was beginning to be concerned for Maralena, Salaman, Mercedes whom I would be driving back to Trenton that night, as we had planned.

Why was I here? Where was this place? A swirl of mad music, strobe lighting, heart-quickening cries and laughter. Some distance away at the slots one of the manic machines had erupted in victory, spewing lights, marching music, tokens. You had to wonder who'd won—had he/she *won big,* or, more likely, *won small.*

Most wins were small. Just enough to keep the machine going.

Most players were losers, in fact. Otherwise, how could a casino keep in business?

I'd known from a Trenton newspaper that most of the Atlantic City casino-hotels, like those in the more prestigious Las Vegas, had had a very bad year. They were hemorrhaging money. Several had filed for bankruptcy. The very Taj Mahal, a landmark on the Boardwalk, was deeply in debt.

Yet, the party continued. The gaiety continued. The gamblers had no sense of the casino as a business enterprise out to exploit their naïveté, no more than they had of fate. It was sobering to me to realize how each day, each night, indistinguishable from one another in the windowless casino in which no clocks were ever displayed, individuals placed themselves at the slot machines, at the blackjack tables, riveted to their immediate transient fates. They were like entranced spirits of Hades—nothing could wake them from their trance except a sudden *win.* It was yet more sobering to see that so many were elderly, walking with difficulty, with canes, or walkers; yet grimly determined to play the slots, to yank the levers, peer at the whirling fruits through bifocal glasses. So many were African-American, a surprise to me. And Asian-American, another surprise.

What a joke! My brother and I squandering what remained of our youth in research into arcane "religious" subjects. How could we imagine that anyone cared, that we could make a serious contribution to our culture that was a fevered casino-culture obsessed with *big wins*?

The pages they'd slapped from my fingers were on the floor, beneath my feet. My fingers groped for them but couldn't pick them up. *How scale walls of Hades?*—the question came unbidden.

I'd had a drink—I'd begun a second drink—confused, that the drinks tasted different.

Somehow, sharing a drink with Mercedes. She'd brought her man-friend to meet me—unless this was a man-friend for *me*. His face looked like a clam's face—if a clam had a face—upon which a dyed-black mustache had been pasted. And what remained of his hair was dyed-black, combed over a lumpy scalp.

"You these girls' *teacher*—somebody said? What kinda class is it, Lyd-ja, you are teaching?" Very funny, the clam-faced man laughed heartily. I saw a nubby glisten inside his mouth, a metal-laced molar.

This man, Mercedes's friend, was trying to escort me somewhere—to the blackjack table? to a nearby bar?—but I managed to wrest my arm loose from his fingers. He cursed me, bluntly. On an escalator I was borne upward—escaping from Clam-Face—the air currents in the Taj were such, I felt the ends of my hair lifting in the breeze—and at the top of the escalator there was an open space, and a brass railing where you could stand to gaze out over the interior of the Taj designed like a bad Indian stage setting, the "Taj Mahal" as imagined by a crude American entrepreneur.

I wanted a microphone! I wanted to be heard! I leaned over the railing waving my arms like a demented semaphore.

"'How scale walls of Hades'! Plato says this is a veil of illusion! A cave of illusions! Delusions! The casino is the cave! You must wake yourself—save your souls!"

A security guard came quickly to lead me away. No one below in the milling casino had heard me—no one had so much as glanced up at me—except my concerned friends Maralena and Salaman who ascended the escalator after me.

Maralena said to the security guard, "Hey man, she just kiddin. She not drunk, hey. Not ust to all this excitement, like—she mostly stay home in Tr'nton. We take care of our girl friend, OK?"

The security guard was tall, well beyond six feet. He wore a uniform that fitted his muscular body like a glove. His face was blunt-boned, his skin as velvety-dark as Leander's. I wanted him to look at me kindly, or at least not with open hostility, but he ignored me entirely speaking to my companions in a low baritone bemused/exasperated tone:

"She is drunk. You think I can't recognize, you' friend is *drunk*? Just keep her from high places. Don't matter what bullshit she be sayin, nobody can hear her anyway. You got me?"

"Thanks man! We appreciate this."

And Salaman said, almost wistfully: "Man you one sweet cool dude."

*   *   *

"I be drivin. Girl, you sleep in the backseat."

Maralena spoke firmly. Though she'd had far more to drink than I had she'd managed to "sober up"—she claimed—with two cups of black coffee.

Coffee! The mere thought turned my stomach.

Maralena and Salaman helped me crawl into the backseat of the Mazda. The vinyl seat cover was icy-cold. How many drinks had I had?—not more than two, or three.

Still, I did not feel—well, "real."

Confused as I'd been falling down the stairs at—what was the name of the residence hall—not Jester College—but another place: where my Newcomb Fellowship provided a room for me—my heel catching in the frayed carpeting on the stairs and I'd plunged down, down . . .

Hello? Are you all right? Let me help you . . .

"How she doin, you think? She ain't ust to drinkin or maybe stayin up late."

"She ain't ust to *nothin much*."

They were laughing at me. Not cruel but affectionate laughter.

Or maybe, slightly ridiculing laughter. Now my wallet was empty of all paper money.

"She pathetic, eh? She just don' *get it*."

"L'nd'r, he like her OK. He say, the white-girl sister is gon be his girl, they get things straight between them."

"What's that mean—'things straight between them'?"

"Fuck how'd I know? L'nd'r ain't even my cousin, he just some boy hangin around my uncle's house, we all growin up."

And they laughed together. No idea why.

It was mean of them to laugh at me when I was helpless.

In the jostling car, on the cold vinyl seat, I kept trying to wake up yet with each effort I fell back into sleep. Trying to explain to a buzzing crowd *How scale walls of—whatever.*

Someone was missing: only three of us in the car hurtling at above the speed limit on the Garden State Parkway in the starless late-night through New Jersey countryside blank and bleak as a cinder wall. For reckless Mercedes had decided to stay a while longer in the casino—she'd connected with a man who'd offered to drive her home in his Jaguar, or maybe he'd rent a room for them, a suite, at the Borgata.

Maralena said, vehement and disapproving, "That *girl*! She gon regret this! Her age, she don't know shit how to handle a man even some old pissy white asshole like that one. You wait, she gon be sorry."

"Her pappy, he gon be damn unhappy. Fuck, I ain't gon mess with *him*."

Now I was worried, Mercedes hadn't come back with us. As the girls' "teacher," I would be blamed for her absence.

If something happened to Mercedes, I would be blamed.

Trying to determine how much money I'd lost that night— tokens I'd gambled away, given away or "loaned"—each time I calculated the sum it was different.

No less than five hundred dollars, certainly. Six hundred?

Next I knew, I was being shaken awake by Maralena—"Lyd'ja! Wake up girl, you *home*."

The car wasn't car-jacked after all. One of my friends had called a relative on her cell, to come pick them up at Grindell Park.

And there was Harvey helping me to walk the stairs. Agitated and disapproving saying words I couldn't decipher, chiding me, cursing me, in Aramaic for all that I knew.

8.

An evil smell in the apartment. Smells.

And whenever I went out, and returned, the contrast between the outdoor air—(even the polluted "outdoor air" of Trenton, New Jersey)—was so extreme, I felt faint stepping into my brother's apartment. *Something has died here. Mice, rats in the walls . . .*

It was always shocking to see, my brother who'd once been over six feet tall, now no taller than I was, and nearly as thin. I slid my arm around his waist to assist his walking and Harvey was resistant at first then unprotesting, ironic. His vertebrae felt loose like marbles caught inside his skin.

Harvey hated the clinic. Hated rehab, and the clinic where he had to submit to "blood work"—two small vials of blood drawn from his veins that had become increasingly shrunken, difficult of access.

These were veins in arms, legs, even feet. In case you thought these were veins merely in Harvey's arms.

In the days following Atlantic City I awaited the wrath of Mercedes's *pappy*. I feared that something had happened to the reckless girl and I would be blamed. I feared that something had happened and I would never see my friends again. Yet I could not bring myself to telephone Maralena on her cell phone, I seemed to know beforehand that my friend had no interest in hearing from me; if I identified myself she would exclaim in her bright vivacious bird-voice *Who? Who that? Sorry you callin a wrong number.*

Must be that I loved my brother, that was why I was here.

Depressing clinic on State Street, Trenton. Not far from Book Bazaar but we had no time for Book Bazaar today.

Welfare, Family Services, Trenton Rescue Mission. Pawnshops and bail-bond shops amid vacant stores on every street. And the white dome of the state capitol building rising above the ruin of the city, less than a mile away, like a luminous cloud.

It was trickery, but also desperation. For ever more that I lived with him, and came to know him, and beneath the patina of his difficult personality, came to love him—I wanted to know my brother's secret for then perhaps I could save his life.

"How's my brother doing, d'you think?"—it was a deceptively casual question put to the nurse at the clinic who might've seen me once or twice before in my brother's company, but didn't really know me; for the medical records of patients are meant to be *confidential,* and Harvey had not ever revealed to me what his medical condition was except he was "anemic"—had some kind of "low blood count." And he'd had some sort of "rehab" that had to be related, I supposed, to drugs. The nurse hesitated before she confided in me, in a lowered voice, and in a way to indicate that she assumed that I already knew these somber facts—

"For HIV patients, it's the medication—how well it works, and how they tolerate it. How their general health is, of course. Your brother has other issues too, you know—he isn't using now, he says, but—he *was*."

For the nurse, it was Harvey's (possible) drug use that was the issue; for me, the stunning news was HIV.

My brother was HIV-positive!

"Yes. You are right. Yes—thank you."

I turned away, not wanting the woman to see tears of anguish welling in my eyes.

Tears of chagrin, disappointment.

Too dazed to sit with rows of patients and their relatives in the crowded and airless waiting room. Better to remain standing, or step outside into the cold air.

Why hadn't I known, or guessed? Why had I wanted to think that Harvey's medical condition was only drugs? And why hadn't Harvey told me? When I'd virtually cast away my life for him.

When Harvey emerged from the interior of the clinic, nearly an hour later, I was still in a state of shock but had taken a seat by this time.

Harvey complained in his affably embittered way of having to be "poked" for the blood work. "Fuck that needle! The tech can't find a vein, God damn makes me feel like a Death Row prisoner they're poking to get the death-IV *in*." Harvey laughed as if he'd said something witty. Then he saw me, blinked and stared at me. "Lydia? You all right?"

"Yes. I am—'all right.'"

"You know, I told you not to come to the clinic with me, I'm perfectly capable of coming here by myself."

"I know. You've said."

Exiting the clinic Harvey was about to propel himself down the steps then wisely hesitated. Wordlessly I slid my arm around his waist, as before.

I'd glimpsed Band-Aids on the insides of both his bruised arms. Very likely there were Band-Aids on the insides of his legs as well, and on his ankles. I would not ask.

Such pity for my brother, such love!—yet it was an angry love.

For Harvey was to blame, I thought—HIV-positive!

No wonder he'd left the seminary, escaped to another life where no one knew him and would not judge him.

No wonder he'd taken up poetry as the most futile gesture of his life.

Quietly I said, guiding his descent down the cement steps, "I don't blame you, Harvey. If anyone is to blame it's me."

A second time, as it was a final time, I returned to Book Bazaar. I yearned to see Wystan again. In my loneliness in Grindell Park—in my fevered imagination—the secondhand bookstore clerk had grown more attractive. I'd forgotten the disheveled hair, the baggy T-shirt and cargo pants—if Wystan's face hovered in my memory it was now blurred with light, like those ghostly figures on TV that are being censored for reasons of privacy, or decency.

Somehow, Wystan was merging with Harvey. With an old memory of Harvey. And hadn't Wystan said that Harvey was a "patrician" of some sort—and so was I; hadn't Wystan said that Harvey was "the most remarkable person" he'd ever met.

The name suggested refinement—"Wystan." And he'd seemed to like me—he'd followed me through the store. He'd hinted at treasures in the basement. He'd tried to acquire my address but, foolishly, I had refused him.

"'Wystan'? He doesn't work here anymore."

A fattish woman of bleak and dissatisfied middle age regarded me suspiciously. In her mouth, "Wystan" had a flat New Jersey twang.

So suspiciously, you would think that a succession of conniving females had trooped into the bookstore, each seeking the elusive Wystan.

"Oh." My disappointment showed in my face, clearly.

"He didn't give notice. Just quit. That is—disappeared. And without closing the store, or calling one of us." The woman spoke with angry reproach, peering at me. "Are you a friend, miss?"

"N-No. I guess—I'm not—a friend . . ."

The woman frowned at me, as if I'd said something particularly stupid. For why would I be looking for the bookstore clerk, if I weren't a friend; and why, if I weren't a friend, was I looking for someone so shabby, so disreputable, so pathetic, and such a loser?

Faltering I asked if she knew where Wystan had gone.

Briskly, and with an air of mean satisfaction, the woman said she had no idea.

Did he work somewhere else? I wondered. In Trenton?

"I've told you, miss—I have no idea."

The woman's curt manner suggested to me that she wasn't a mere employee, as Wystan had been. Not the owner of the store, or a manager but—more likely—the disgruntled wife of the owner.

Though I understood it was hopeless to try to engage the woman in any sort of exchange I heard myself asking, doggedly: "When did he leave the store?"

"'Leave the store'? I have no idea."

The obfuscatory way in which the woman spoke was bewildering to me. There was a secret here, a subtext.

I thought *Wystan has not left the store. He disappeared into the basement—into the books. No one has seen him since.*

Though she had not been very helpful I thanked the woman politely. It is one of the principles of my social behavior that I try not to repay rudeness with more rudeness; I try to repay ill-treatment with a friendly smile, or at least a neutral smile.

Under the woman's dubious gaze I made my way to the Religion/Anthropology shelves as if drawn by a magnet. It was a shock—not a good shock—to see a copy of the bound galley of *Cleansing Rituals: Mother, Infant, Taboo*—the doctoral dissertation published by the University of California Press which I'd been assigned to review, but had not reviewed. I felt a touch of vertigo, that a rival had so bypassed me.

At the cashier's counter the woman was squinting in my direction. As if to confound her suspicions of me I selected two paperbacks—*God of the Oppressed* and *The Hermeneutics of Desire*.

But I wasn't yet ready to leave Book Bazaar. My heartbeat quickened as I approached the stairs to the basement. Slowly I descended, step by step. I knew, or seemed to know—Wystan was there, in some way.

As he'd told me, the large, narrow, cave-like room was filled with books—boxes, cartons, and shopping bags filled with books, floor-to-ceiling shelves of books, books stacked on the floor. Against one wall were rows of flattened cardboard boxes and emptied cartons. The air was close and smelled of dust, grime, Time—a faint odor that reminded me of my brother's apartment, especially on humid days.

Softly I whispered, "Wystan? Hello? It's Lydia—a friend . . ."

My eye was drawn to a farther corner of the cavernous room where the walls had become indistinct, as if dissolved in shadow; as if the dark earth beyond were pressing inward. There was a kind of pressure here, I felt—an indefinable yet palpable pressure.

Cautiously I stepped away from the stairs. There were narrow pathways between partially unpacked boxes and cartons. How like a graveyard the room was, dimly lit by tremulous fluorescent lights overhead. Wystan had remarked that he'd heard voices here, whispers—he'd figured at the periphery of his vision. I steeled myself for these also but saw and heard nothing except the muffled sounds of traffic outside the grimy basement windows.

I waited, scarcely breathing. Though Wystan didn't reveal himself to me, I felt his presence. Almost, I saw the man's face—a familiar homely-but-beloved face like that of a relative who is rarely seen yet nonetheless exerts an abiding spell over you.

There was a sound of footsteps, the creaking floor overhead. As if someone were walking there, approaching the opened door to the stairs.

Quickly I whispered, "Wystan? Good-bye. I think—I guess—I won't be coming back . . ."

There was a sound at the top of the stairs: the fattish middle-aged woman, suspicious of me.

Was I rummaging through cartons looking for rare, signed first editions; was I going to hide a precious book inside my coat; was I to be trusted, who looked so furtive?

The flat nasal New Jersey voice called down to me: "Can I help you, miss? Are you looking for anything in particular? Books in the basement haven't been sorted and categorized yet, so we prefer that customers not come down here."

I returned to the ground floor. I made an effort to smile at the glowering woman who rang up my modest purchases on an old-fashioned cash register with an air of scarcely concealed impatience. I realized that she resented her life, she resented and hated books. *She is not someone's wife but someone's left-behind wife. She too has been abandoned to the book graveyard.*

With my few remaining low-denomination bills I paid for my books thinking with what pleasure I would read them, as if Wystan himself had pressed them into my hand.

*   *   *

Like a large white finely cracked egg Harvey's secret lay between us.

The egg in the swans' nest. Just visibly cracked, containing death and decay and not a fuzzy little cygnet.

But when will the swans acknowledge the death-egg? Is it possible to choose a specific hour, a moment, when such an irrevocable truth must be uttered?

Swans mate for life, it's said. A sister and a brother too are "mated for life"—irrevocably, by blood.

Harvey would not reveal his secret to me, I knew. Nor could I reveal Harvey's secret to him—that I knew it.

Did we love each other enough, to withstand such a secret? Or did we love each other too much, to withstand such a secret?

For the first time in a very long time, I called my parents—tried to call my parents. But a recording clicked on: *This number has been disconnected.*

Disconnected! I was shocked, and puzzled.

I called one of my sisters who told me that of course our parents' phone was disconnected—they'd made a big move, surely they'd told me about it?—to Orlando, Florida.

Big move? Orlando? I knew nothing of this.

"They're living in a 'gated retirement community'—'no children allowed.' I've seen pictures on the Internet, but we haven't visited them yet. Haven't been invited." My sister laughed in that rueful way in which we'd learned to laugh, speaking of our parents.

I was stunned by this news. I felt betrayed by this news.

I hung up the phone, not knowing what I'd said to my sister, or if I'd said anything coherent at all.

Guess where our parents are! I wanted to goad Harvey.

Guess who has abandoned us, in Trenton!

Of course, I never said a word to my brother.

Days had passed. Eventually, weeks.

I had failed to reply to Professor A.'s email and to several emails from the director of the Newcomb program. Emails to me from these individuals had ceased.

And so, one day I set out on a journey: to drive to the fabled University sixty miles to the north.

The distance was *not far*. Yet, my uneasiness was such, the distance felt *very far*.

Much of the drive would be along Route 1. I consoled myself, it would not take more than an hour.

I tried to rehearse what I would say to Professor A. What I would say about my "progress" in translating the Eweian manuscript, and when I believed I might finish it. How I believed I would be interpreting the material in my thesis. *I don't agree with you at all, Professor A. I think you are an old fool and utterly mistaken. But I want your imprimatur on my thesis, Professor. I want your blessing.*

So too, my imagined words put to the director of the Newcomb program, were upsetting to me. *I want the University's money, that is all I want. The rest is bullshit.*

I had to have faith, more inspired words would come to me, as soon as I stepped onto the idyllic University campus that floated like a fairy-world just slightly above the polluted soil and waters of New Jersey.

Yet soon then it happened, after leaving the Grindell Park neighborhood, I became lost on Trenton's one-way streets. Twenty minutes were required to get to Camden Avenue, to which I could have walked in half that time! But once I was on Camden Avenue, some miles north I decided to turn onto Route 206, thinking that this would be a sort of shortcut, but then, somehow, I found myself routed into driving south instead of north—when I realized my mistake I was being shunted over a bridge crossing the Delaware River into Pennsylvania.

By the time I exited, and returned to New Jersey, I was feeling very agitated. Worries about my brother's health assailed me, and thoughts of Maralena, from whom I hadn't heard since our trip to Atlantic City, though she and her friends owed me a considerable amount of money . . . At last I found myself turning onto Route 1 north; but shortly afterward, in a rush of thunderous truck-traffic, I was unable to change lanes out of an exit-only lane for Interstate 95, south toward Philadelphia.

Philadelphia! Always I seemed to be routed south, when I wanted to drive north.

Finally, I managed to exit the crowded interstate, and enter rushing traffic on Route 1 north. But by this time my head pounded with pain. A powerful yearning rose in me, to exit the state highway at Camden Avenue, and make my way home.

That is what I did, that day.

Harvey seemed annoyed to see me. Or maybe his grimace was meant to signal concern.

"Back so soon? I thought you were going to meet with your dissertation advisor . . ."

I couldn't bear my brother's jeering, mock-concern. I staggered into my bedroom and fell onto the sofa.

He wants to see me humbled. But if I am broken entirely, he will have no one.

Another day, a brightly sunny day that became inexplicably riddled with storm clouds within a few minutes after I left Grindell Park, I retraced my original route to Route 1 north; I drove with care, remaining in the right lane despite impatient drivers behind me; but once I left Trenton, in the suburb of Lawrenceville, I seem to have made an error exiting, and was shunted around a gigantic cloverleaf that took me, like a transfixed child strapped in an amusement ride, to a gigantic mall—Quaker Bridge! Streams of traffic passed my car on both sides. I could not even see the highway any longer, nor guess where it was. In the parking lot behind a gigantic JCPenney's I gripped the steering wheel and laid my head on my arms trying not to cry.

They are taking my fellowship from me. My career. They will deny that they know me. I am being peeled away from them, picked off their skin like lice.

It was that day, or that evening, that, returning to my brother's apartment, I realized that the smell of rot had grown stronger.

Though I had not been gone for many hours, the apartment seemed to have been visited. My housekeeping had been confounded —the kitchen counters I'd cleaned were now sticky with spilled liquid, chairs were out of place in the kitchen and in the living room. Strangers had forced their way into my brother's life, selling and buying dope. He had all but admitted it to me—he was helpless to keep the drug dealers out of his apartment that was, to them, so convenient a setting for drug deals. They had other residences in Trenton, they did not return to the same place for as long as a week sometimes, but they always returned. The smells of male perspiration, tobacco smoke, marijuana (?), hashish (?), beer, decay and rot made my nostrils constrict; turned my stomach; caused my head to ache. The futile effort to drive to the University had left me broken and defeated and there was Harvey sprawled in a ratty easy chair in the living room scribbling into his notebook. His hands were skeletal, but his fingers moved swiftly gripping a pen. His eyes were heavy-lidded, red-lidded. His lips were covered in scabs I had not noticed before. I shuddered to see that the smallest finger on his right hand was freshly bandaged—now, little more than a stub.

"Harvey? What is that terrible smell? How can you stand it . . ."

" 'Smell'? 'Small smell quells all'—a haiku."

"Has something died in here? Inside a wall?"

" 'Small smell quells all—inside a wall.' No good."

"We should open the windows, at least. We should try to find the source of the smell."

"An experimental haiku, I meant. A classical haiku has seventeen syllables."

Maddening Harvey! He smelled the sickening odor of course but lacked the energy, volition, desire to seek out the source.

There were only a few pieces of furniture in the living room. The easy chair in which Harvey sprawled, and several other chairs; a two-cushion sofa, of badly worn leather, upon which Leander and Tin usually sat when they came to the apartment— (Leander to the right, Tin to the left, invariably). There were scattered tables, lamps of which at least one was unplugged.

The leather sofa had been shoved oddly into a corner, since I'd left the apartment. But behind the sofa, just visible from an angle, was what appeared to be a length of rolled-up carpet.

As I approached the carpet, the smell grew stronger. It was unmistakable now—organic decay, rot.

"Harvey? What is this? Something against the wall . . ."

I was having difficulty breathing, the smell was so strong.

Clumsily I pushed the sofa aside. For a small piece of furniture, it was heavy; and Harvey made no offer to help.

I squatted over the rolled-up carpet. Holding my breath until my head spun. Desperately I managed to tug off a length of twine that had been securing the rug. (This was a rug that had been on the floor of Harvey's bedroom when I'd first arrived.) Boldly, recklessly I managed to tug off the other length of twine, and to unroll the carpet—and there, arms stretched above his head, flat yellowish face dull as a much-worn coin and his eyes and mouth gaping open like a fish's, was Leander's lieutenant Tin.

Tin's flaccid torso was covered in a blood-soaked, dried-bloody T-shirt. He'd been shot, perhaps—or stabbed . . .

He didn't look young now. Something terrible had happened to Tin's face, straining the skin to bursting.

I screamed and stumbled back. I screamed and stumbled to Harvey. With a look of profound exasperation Harvey was regarding me as one might regard a lunatic. He'd had to set down his notebook and place his pen in his shirt pocket. As a schoolboy, Harvey was never without a pen or a pencil in his shirt pocket. In a disapproving voice he said, "God damn, Lydia—I told you not to look. Whatever you've found—it's none of your concern. Just *stop*."

"It's Tin—he's dead. It's Tin's body, rolled up in your carpet. We have to call the police . . ."

Harvey cursed me in a lowered voice. In moments of acute exasperation he lapsed into one of his ancient, extinct languages—might've been Aramaic, Sanskrit or Greek. He said, "I told you this was not a good idea, Lydia—living here with me. I warned you it was not a good environment for you. I said—*stay away*. And now."

"Harvey, my God! We have to call the p-police . . . Tin is dead, Tin is behind the sofa, somebody has shot Tin in our apartment . . ."

"There were no gunshots, that I heard. And we will not 'call the police.' No."

"A man has been murdered, in our apartment. We have to call the police . . ."

Sighing, Harvey swung himself out of the easy chair, that had sunken and shaped itself to his buttocks. It was always startling to me, that my brother had grown so *short*.

We would re-fit Tin's heavy body into the blood-soaked interior of the carpet roll exactly as it had been fitted previously. We would re-roll the carpet and secure the ends with twine. Clearly, others had addressed the logistics of this problem, or the first stage of the problem; we could not have improved upon their method, and did not try. When Harvey did not respond to my desperate words, my emotion and my tears, I fell silent—like Harvey.

Had Tin's body been in the apartment, without my knowing? Since when—the previous day? Two days? It had not seemed that he'd been murdered recently. The blood had ceased flowing, and had partially dried. Poor Tin! He'd looked at me with an expression of inarticulate longing, from time to time. Yet he'd never once uttered my name.

Now, it was too late.

"This problem would've been dealt with, Lydia, without your interference. But now you've interfered . . ."

I had no idea what Harvey was saying. His voice was edgy, not so calm as he'd tried to suggest; his jaws were trembling, as with a spell of extreme cold.

When it was sufficiently night, when Grindell Park was more or less vacated of dealers and customers and only a few homeless bundles of rags slept on the benches, and wouldn't give so much as a glance to two figures struggling to drag a strangely heavy length of rolled-up carpet across the desiccated grass, we managed to transport Tin's body into the most remote corner of the park where we hid it amid debris from tree cuttings, as children might try to hide something from the eyes of their elders.

"The freezing air will impede the decay. The Trenton police won't be able to calculate when he died, or where."

Harvey spoke shrewdly, as if this were a statement of fact he'd had occasion to pronounce in the past.

When we returned to the apartment it was nearly 4 A.M. In two hours, it would be dawn. Though we were exhausted and light-headed we took time to open all the windows, in my bedroom and in Harvey's bedroom as well. Not soon, but eventually, the putrid odor would fade. Or, the putrid odor would mingle with other, near-similar odors in the old house as in the air of Trenton, New Jersey—smells of smoldering rubber, diesel exhaust from giant rigs lumbering along Camden Avenue, the toxic-sweet odors from chemical companies long extinct. And one balmy April afternoon when I was returning from Shop-Rite, on a crumbling Camden Avenue sidewalk there stood a brash young man with dreadlocks tumbling down his back and a Maori tattoo on half his face, a velvety-dark-skinned Leander who sighting me shot out his hand, his large thumb, to hitch a ride with me in the Mazda—(only with me, his friend Lydia, for he hadn't been hitchhiking a moment before, I was sure)—and shrewdly I thought *Oh no! not a chance* even as my car braked to a stop, yes it was too late, yes but it was an instinctive involuntary gesture and so I heard myself say as Leander in tight-fitting suede deep-purple jacket, vest, trousers opened the passenger's door and slid his long legs inside with a wide grin and an air of companionable ease—"Well, all right. I can give you a ride. But I'm not going farther than Grindell Park."

The Last Man of Letters

It was a season of numerous discontents. The more acclaimed X was, the more the myriad imperfections of others offended him. The imperfections of women, particularly.

There were women who offended by making no effort to be feminine—sexually attractive. There were women who offended by making too obvious an effort. As if he, aged seventy-three, were an ordinary old fool, a would-be lecher to be galvanized into responding to female subterfuge of any kind.

X had become by degrees an elder literary celebrity of international reputation, a novelist, poet and essayist once called by the *Times Literary Supplement* the "last man of letters"—an exaggeration surely, but one which pleased. He was a perennial candidate for a Nobel Prize, a favorite of many outspoken literary commentators in England and the United States. In real life he was larger, more bulky of body than his photographs suggested; still he had a handsome head, a much-creased but lapidary face with recessed, hooded, haunted-looking eyes, thin white hair brushed back from his forehead in wings. He smiled rarely; his face had grown mask-like with thought, calculation. His manners were exquisite, though sometimes rather rude. He was, his admirers acknowledged, difficult. But a genius of course. Even before he'd become rich he'd taken care to dress expensively in custom-made suits, perfectly starched white cotton shirts, elegant neckties. His nails were manicured, his jaws always smoothly shaven, his cologne carefully chosen. There had emerged in the past several months a just-perceptible, infuriating tremor in his left hand which X controlled by gripping that hand tightly whenever possible. And sometimes, in the early morning, his eyes watered mysteriously, blurring his vision in a maddening way as if his eyes were unprepared, after the intense, private state of sleep, for contact with the air. But X had never been one to indulge weakness in himself or in others, and he gave little thought to these matters. Because he'd become famous, he was much photographed; because much photographed he became yet more famous. Often he murmured his name aloud—*X. I am he, I am X and no other*. He could not have said if he was proud of such a fate, or humble. From within, the great man may be as much in awe of his greatness as are others. *How has it happened—I am X.* These were secrets of X's inner life of course. Never shared with another.

Another secret, X could not keep from sharing with certain others: his several wives, and those women with whom, over the decades, he'd become intimate. This was his asthmatic condition, which he'd endured through more than six decades. The attacks varied widely in intensity, having been very severe in childhood, intermittently so in adulthood and now more or less controlled by medication developed in the last twenty years. Yet sometimes in the middle of the night X woke choking for breath, thrashing about in terror that breath would be denied him—his life would be denied him! He'd badly frightened his most recent wife, shortly before leaving on an ambitious European tour to promote his newest book, when he'd wakened from a seemingly dreamless sleep convinced he was choking, suffocating. The woman sharing his bed, whom he had not immediately recognized as his wife, had cried, panicked, "What is it? Oh, what is it?"—but even after he'd recovered from the attack, X didn't tell her his secret since childhood. *I'm fighting for my life.*

Strange, how he took an instant, visceral dislike to the girl. Her incessant, nervous smile in his presence. Her fleshy lips that were too pale, without lipstick. A plain scrubbed-looking face devoid of makeup. How like a schoolgirl in manner, shy, eager to please, yet her khaki-colored clothes, a loose-fitting jacket and matching trousers, her lean, boyish body itself seemed to him brazenly unappealing. This girl was of any age between twenty and thirty, he supposed; it offended him, that his French publisher had chosen her to translate his latest book of essays. In the publisher's office he'd barely nodded at her when they were introduced, and had not heard her last name; it was unclear by his manner whether in fact he understood she was his translator; there was that way about X, an aristocratic hauteur even as he smiled, uttered witticisms, spoke at length and always compellingly, as if his words were prose and not merely words. At the luncheon in his honor, in an elegant four-star Parisian restaurant, he'd avoided sitting anywhere near the unattractive girl in khaki, and had not once glanced at her during the course of the meal; yet he heard himself saying coldly, in response to some praise of his new book made by one of the journalists at the table, "Really! But the translation leaves something to be desired, I think? I open the book at random, and I read—" And in his beautifully modulated voice, clear enough to be heard virtually everywhere in the restaurant, X read a passage with seeming spontaneity and subtle, almost playful mockery, in the translator's French; then shut his eyes and recited his own prose, in English. Around the table, his audience of twelve people sat very still, listening in amazement. What a performance! How it would be spoken of, for years afterward! Not once did X glance at the girl-translator who, stricken with chagrin, sat hunched gracelessly forward, elbows on the table and both hands pressed against her mouth. X was a gentleman yet could not mitigate his scorn. "There is no excuse, I think we can agree, for such slovenliness," he said, and shut the book with a snap.

In the embarrassed silence, the girl-translator murmured something dazed and unintelligible, whether in English or in French X could not have said, and stumbled away from the table.

X's publisher began to apologize profusely, of course. As did others at the firm. It would require many minutes, and a fresh bottle of 1962 Bordeaux, to bring the distinguished man of letters around to his usual equanimity.

*   *   *

You won't readily forget X, will you, my girl? Alone in his luxurious hotel suite, mellow with the afterglow of exquisite wine, X felt a belated tinge of guilt. Seeing again the girl-translator's plain, pale face, the fading smile and that look of slow-dawning incredulity and hurt in her eyes. Though it had seemed dramatically spontaneous, X's gesture had been rehearsed; in fact he'd had to search for some minutes before the luncheon, to find a passage from the French edition of his book that might seem to diverge slightly in tone from the original English. (X wondered if perhaps he'd done something like this before, in another language, during an earlier European tour? His performance seemed to him vaguely familiar, like the startled expressions on the faces of his rapt listeners.) He smiled uneasily, thinking of how the tale would be told, and retold, in literary Paris. Swiftly it would make its way to London, and New York. X's French publisher had promised that, in future editions of X's book, the offensive passage would be modified; the several journalists at the luncheon, attached to major Parisian publications, would respectfully report X's penchant for perfectionism. Almost, X felt sorry for the girl-translator. She was young, inexperienced, ignorant. It hadn't been entirely her fault, perhaps.

For after all X had a reputation to uphold. *The last man of letters.*

En route to Berlin several days later, X inwardly vowed he wouldn't behave in such a way again, no matter how provoked, for after all he was a gentleman, yet soon after his arrival, during a press conference at his hotel, he found himself another time repelled by a young female—a striking blond journalist attached to the cultural desk of one of Germany's premiere weekly magazines. This girl-journalist was younger even than the French girl-translator, or appeared so; considerably younger than the other interviewers, who were nearly all men. X found it difficult to take his eyes off her even when he was answering questions put to him by others; for here was a brazenly attractive female, no doubt one of the new-generation Berliners of whom X had heard who were professionally ambitious and sexually liberated. Here was a girl well aware of the impression she made upon male eyes. She had long straight dyed-blond hair that fell past her shoulders, and large, staring eyes behind green-tinted glasses, and full, fleshy lips that shone with crimson gloss; she was forever moving her body seductively, and brushing her hair out of her eyes with nervous gestures, and fixing X with a gaze of starstruck adulation so extreme as to seem mocking. And how absurd her costume, resembling a parachutist's jumpsuit of some silvery-steel synthetic fabric, clinging to a thin, perversely erotic body. X felt a shiver of repugnance that a female so blatantly lacking both breasts and hips should present herself in a seductive manner. And her Berliner-accented English grated against his ears. And she was hardly shy, posing questions with the confidence, or more than the confidence, of her fellow interviewers. How did she dare! The girl seemed to pride herself on her ability to speak English, allowing X to know that she traveled often to the United States and had stayed for some time in New York—"in TriBeCa"; and she'd read "almost every one" of X's books as a college student, in English of course. X stared at the girl-interviewer with scarcely concealed fury. There was a tremor in his left eye, and he was obliged to grip his left hand tightly with his right; someone must have been smoking in the room, for his throat was constricted. How offensive, the way the girl-interviewer wetted her lips as she posed a question of X; brushing her shining hair out of her face for the dozenth time, and leaning forward so that the neck of the jumpsuit shifted to reveal the tops of her small waxy-white breasts, naked inside the costume. Worse yet, she had a way of uttering X's full name with heavily accented solemnity as if the distinguished man of letters were already dead, and this were some sort of posthumous occasion honoring him. Unbearable! At last X lost his patience, startling everyone in the room by bringing his fist down hard on a tabletop, and saying, with icy courtesy, "Excuse me, fraulein. Would you please speak English? I am having a most difficult time understanding you."

X had interrupted the blond girl-interviewer in the midst of a lengthy, pretentious question about X's literary forebears and his political leanings, and now she blinked at him in stunned chagrin, startled as if he'd leaned over to slap her arrogant face. There was an abrupt silence in the room. (It seemed to X that the other interviewers glanced at one another with small smiles— they approved, did they, of X's admonishment?) A half-dozen tape cassettes spun in their machines in the awkward stillness.

Then the girl stammered an apology, her face flushed; the press conference resumed, though with more formality and hesitancy; no one wished to offend X, but posed to him questions of a sort he encountered everywhere in Europe, to which he answered with his usual balance of wit and sobriety, casualness and elegance. At the conclusion of the hour everyone applauded; everyone, with the conspicuous exception of the blond girl who'd sat silent and hunched in her chair as others spoke, staring at X's feet, twisting a strand of hair and bringing it to her mouth unconsciously, like an overgrown, hurt child. As the others politely shook X's hand in farewell, and thanked him for the privilege of the interview, the girl retreated without a word, and was gone. X frowned after her, annoyed. It would only have been good manners for her to come forward and apologize, after all.

It was clear that the new generation of German youth lacked the courtesy of their elders. X had noticed, too, belatedly, with a small tinge of regret, that the girl had brought with her a tote bag no doubt crammed with books of X's she'd hoped for him to sign; but she'd crept away without asking him to sign even one. So rude.

Also in Berlin, X was vexed by the publicist assigned to him during his visit, a fleshy, perfumy girl in an alarmingly short vinyl mini-skirt, black-textured stockings and shiny black boots to mid-thigh, who, in the limousine in which they traveled together from appointment to appointment, was forever chattering on her cellular phone; yet he maintained a dignified composure, and made no complaint of her apart from a casual, glancing remark to the head of the publishing house, about the amusing resemblance between the professional class of young Berlin women and "women for hire"; for in Berlin, as through Germany, X was treated with the respect due one of his stature; as his German agent pointed out, sales of X's books were high, and steady. In Stockholm, Copenhagen, in Amsterdam, and at last in Rome, at the conclusion of his itinerary, X was treated royally, and so made an effort to bear in stoical silence, as much as he could, the grating imperfections of girl-translators, girl-interviewers, girl-publicists and even, outrageously, girl-editors—for it was quite a shock to X, to discover that the editor at his Italian publisher who'd overseen his books for twenty years had retired and been replaced by an exuberant young Milanese woman of no more than thirty-five; a specialist in American literature who'd taken courses at Columbia and whose name was something like Tonia, or Tanya. X took an immediate dislike to this girl-editor whose complexion appeared slightly coarse, and whose long face and nose were so recognizably Italian; he disapproved of makeup in one so homely, and wondered if the single gold ring on her left hand was a wedding band—or was X supposed to play a sort of guessing game, not knowing if she was married or not? Though Tonia, or Tanya, was deferential to the elder distinguished writer, he resented her familiarity with his books as if, knowing his books, she somehow knew *him*; forever quoting, in the presence of others, from X's writing, as if he were a revered authority on literature, politics, morals, the very universe. Nothing more vulgar than fulsome flattery!

Almost, X wondered that Tonia, or Tanya, was deliberately making him out to be, by her excessive homage, a pompous old fool? "Enough please!" X several times protested, but his distress was misinterpreted by the girl as old-fashioned humility, or shyness; she persisted in her enthusiasm, until X had all he could do to listen in pained silence. It annoyed him, too, that Tonia, or Tanya, should exhibit such a general zest for American writers, including on her list even notorious feminists who had, for political reasons, long ago denounced X. Had she no sense? Had she no embarrassment? X was particularly incensed when she introduced him as "the greatest American writer of his generation." *American, only! Of his generation, only!* As if X's achievement had not lifted him well above the merely provincial and time-bound. X felt the sting of this insult as if the arrogant young woman had reached over to tweak his nose; but he bore his displeasure in dignified silence until at last, on the eve of his departure from Rome, at a small, elegant dinner in his honor, when the girl-editor began again to quote him in her proprietary, maddening way, to his host, the wealthy owner of the publishing house, he said, in a voice clear and penetrating enough to be heard about the table, "Excuse me! I am so very weary of chattering sycophants, I believe I would like to be driven to my hotel."

How silent everyone was, at once. How like magic, X's effect upon these strangers. He did not deign to glance at the stunned girl-editor but was well aware of the incredulity and hurt in her eyes.

And so, dramatically, there came to an end X's European itinerary, the last publicity tour of his career.

You won't readily forget X, will you, my girl?

X smiled to himself as, in his luxurious hotel suite at the top of the Spanish Steps, he prepared somewhat distractedly for bed, and for an early awakening in the morning. Yet he was incensed, still; insulted; his dinner hadn't agreed with him, nor the several glasses of Chianti; an artery throbbed in his head, and his breath was short as if he'd been running. The indignities he'd had to bear on this European trip, outrageous for one of his stature and age! No doubt there was, in his wake, a flurry of anecdotes, in time to become literary legends; much would be embellished, and exaggerated. But such was unavoidable, for X was after all a famous man; about famous men, all sorts of wild legends accrue; he was an artist, a creator; like Picasso, Beethoven—a man of unpredictable moods; a man of genius, of course; and genius must be indulged, not stifled.

X had been driven back to the hotel in his host's limousine, accompanied by the contrite, apologetic man, and though X had of course accepted his publisher's apologies for the tactless behavior of an employee, X was well aware that the girl-editor herself had retreated from the table in mortified silence, no doubt to a women's room to repair the damage done to her vanity; but she'd made no effort to follow after X, to explain and to apologize. X wondered if it might be time to instruct his Italian agent to find another publisher for his books, one more congenial to his needs?

So you will see, X is not to be treated lightly.

This prospect would ordinarily have placated X, for through his career he'd derived considerable pleasure from making abrupt switches from publisher to publisher, and indeed he'd switched literary agents several times; but, happening to turn on an overhead fluorescent light in his bathroom which he hadn't turned on previously, he was shocked to see how exhausted, how sallow, how aged he looked. *Is that X? I? Dear God!* X's heart thudded as if a cruel prank had been played on him. Like many individuals of a certain age, he had long practiced the technique of what might be called selective scrutiny; rarely did he approach a mirror head-on, but at a discreet angle; he seemed to know by instinct which mirrors would glare out at him, and which would soothe his eyes; in his imagination, it was not a mirror-reflection he saw when picturing himself, but his most frequently reprinted publicity photograph, which showed a handsome white-haired gentleman with sensitive eyes, a wide, thought-creased brow, and a sympathetic expression. But, now, in the bathroom mirror, what did he see but a ghastly frog-face, sunken eyes and quivering jowls and a pug nose with dark, hairy nostrils! Is that X? *No, it cannot be.* All along others, including women, had gazed openly upon this face, while he himself had been spared; but now he saw his own true face, in the fluorescent glare of a bathroom mirror in Rome, and the sight of it made him sway with dizziness, nausea. He slammed the flat of his hand against the mirror and cried, "I deserve better. I deserve your respect. How dare you insult me!"

*   *   *

Though X was exhausted, as exhausted as he'd ever been in his life, and though the enormous canopied bed was as comfortable a bed as he'd ever lain in, he had difficulty sleeping; his brain swirled with vivid, hallucinatory images and shrill snatches of voices and laughter; his dinner weighed heavily in his stomach, and the wine he'd drunk, against doctor's orders, for X took blood-pressure medication, made his temples ache and his heart pound in a wayward, lurching manner. As often at such times when, in a foreign city, amid luxurious surroundings, he was suffused with a sense of regret, melancholy, guilt; for what exactly, he didn't know; for having quarreled with his wife, perhaps, before leaving on the tour; for having refused to take her with him; even as, in his confused state, he had to acknowledge that he didn't clearly recall which wife, which woman, this was; on a previous European tour he'd fallen in love with a woman some years younger than he, and he'd divorced his wife to marry this woman, but precisely which woman she was, and whether she preceded, or succeeded, one or two other women who resembled her, he didn't know; the effort of trying to make sense of it exhausted him, and disgusted him. *What do I care for the merely personal life? I am destined for higher things.* With a start he recalled that he had children scattered about the world, not only grown but frankly middle-aged children, and there was something repulsive about middle-aged children, something very unnatural; could he be responsible for squabbling offspring, must he be their father forever? Why should he, X, who'd labored so hard to create a reputation, to amass a modest fortune, provide them with the charity they seemed to think they deserved? As if, crouched forever in X's shadow, deprived of natural sunshine, these hulking, overgrown children possessed no volition of their own, no souls. *Leave me alone! I don't know a single one of you.*

Suddenly the dark of the unfamiliar bedroom was shattered by a gaily ringing phone close beside X's bed. X fumbled to answer, stunned, groggy, yet relieved, for he'd had enough of his miserable thoughts; this was his last night in Rome, his last night in Europe, and he deserved better; the call was from the hotel room service, a heavily accented Italian voice inquiring if the signore would accept a midnight treat from admirers of his books; X heard himself say, with childlike eagerness, "Yes, good! Send it up, please, at once." Though the suite was already filled with virtually untouched gifts, bottles of wine, champagne, liqueur, expensive pâté and cheeses, as well as enormous, cloyingly fragrant floral displays of the kind suitable for a funeral home. Quickly X climbed out of bed, struggled into his silk dressing gown, squinted into a mirror and made a swipe at brushing back his disheveled, filmy-pale hair from his flushed forehead. Here was a more flattering mirror, softened by lamplight, providing a more authentic portrait of the elder distinguished writer. Even as X stumbled into the other room he heard a low rapid knocking at the door, for already the room service delivery was there; he heard, too, curious muffled voices and giggles in the corridor. Excitedly he called, "Yes, thank you, I'm here!"

Opening the door then to see to his surprise that the bellboy was not a male after all, but a female: though wearing the old-fashioned olive-gray livery of the renowned hotel, with rows of buttons and gold brocade, and a visored cap perched rakishly on her head. Why, it was the girl-editor of X's Italian publishing house whom, only an hour or so ago, X had denounced as a chattering sycophant! Tonia, or Tanya, clearly wanted to make restitution, to apologize; her skin was no longer coarse and displeasing to the eye but glowed with cosmetics and her thick black Italian-looking hair was loose, in tendrils and wisps falling seductively to her shoulders.

Even as, in exuberant high spirits Tonia, or Tanya, flashed a dazzling smile at the elder writer, crying, "Signore X, may we come in? We have such surprises!" X understood that he would forgive her.

How dreamlike and confused and deliriously wonderful it was, X's surprise midnight treat, like nothing else X had ever experienced in more than seventy years of existence: and only a few minutes before, how self-pitying, how morbid he had been! He stood back in awe as the Italian girl-editor and another attractive female in bellboy livery pushed an ornate silver cart of the approximate size of a hospital gurney into the sitting room: the cart was heaped with delicacies—an unusually large bottle of champagne, in a gilt-embossed wrapper not familiar to X's eye, goose-liver pâté and gourmet cheeses and crusty breads, chocolate-covered truffles, bonbons, cashews and pistachio nuts, and remarkable fruits of all varieties, great glossy apples,

blood-oranges, fat black grapes, plums and kiwis, classically pro-
portioned and in colors vivid as a still life by Matisse. X saw to
his astonishment that the Italian girl's companion was the German fraulein with the long shimmering dyed-blond hair who'd
interviewed him in Berlin!—the first several buttons of her jacket
were unbuttoned to show the alluring tops of her pale, perfect
little breasts, and she too flashed a dazzling smile at X, as if she
and he were old friends, sharing delicious secrets. At once, his
heart swelling with magnanimity, X forgave the brash fraulein,
too. "Yes, of course! Please come in," he stammered, laughing in
delight. It occurred to X that, through his long blessed life, in
such instances of surprise and confusion, he'd stood by helplessly
as others, nearly always women, took charge.

And now a third young female in bellboy costume appeared,
helping to push the cart, and yet a fourth! The heavy door was
shut, and discreetly double-locked, amid giggles high-pitched
and silvery as the tinkling of ice cubes in delicate crystal gob-
lets. X tried to behave as if he were not astonished but perhaps
halfway accustomed to such episodes of high gleefulness; he
clapped robustly, laughing; what did he care that he would be
awakened by a call at 6:30 A.M., to be driven to the airport; what
did he care for mere sleep, he who had often stayed up through
the night working at his books, and sometimes, though less
frequently, making vigorous love.

Already the girls had taken over the sitting room, there was the
German publicist with the full, shapely perfumy body, there was
the French girl-translator he'd misjudged as plain, graceless and

without charm, quite transformed now, with rouged cheeks and lips, mischievously shining eyes, and a ripe body that strained at the silk fabric of her costume. With giggles, X was pushed onto a sofa; with the jarring sound of an artery popping, the enormous champagne bottle was uncorked; the ebullient Italian girl splashed champagne into a long-stemmed glass for X, and into glasses for herself and her companions, and she raised her glass in a toast, declaring that this midnight feast was in homage to a great writer, to the last man of letters, whose work had penetrated their souls and changed their lives permanently—"Signore X, thank you!" Breathless, X drank from his glass; the champagne was delicious, though slightly tart, with a queer metallic bouquet; its myriad miniature bubbles flew up his nostrils and into his brain, to burst. More toasts followed, for the girls were insatiable in their praise of X, he begged them, "Please, please! Enough! You are very kind, but—" and they crowded in to kiss him, wild wet kisses landing anywhere, one of the German girls cried, "Ah, no, Herr X, we are not kind at all, we are only just . . ." Though X tried to push their hands away, the girls prepared him for the feast like a great baby, tucking a linen napkin beneath his chin; the French girl patted him familiarly up and down his sides, and gave his cheek a caress; another girl bestowed a wet smacking kiss on his right ear, and another girl bestowed a wet smacking kiss on the dome of his head; more champagne was splashed into glasses, and drunk; champagne ran in rivulets down X's chin, and wetted the linen napkin; X understood that this was a game, perhaps it was a game he'd played in the past, a celebration of his worth: he, the male, was the girls' captive, their trophy: they were his preening captors, but also his adoring slaves.

Next, they competed with one another to ply X with delicacies from the silver cart: an apple pared and sliced into bite-sized pieces; pâté lavishly smeared on a piece of crusty bread; a large chocolate-covered truffle. To his surprise, X was hungry after all, ravenously hungry, his angel-girls had aroused his long-dulled appetite, tears glistened in his eyes as he ate, he squirmed on the sofa wracked with delight as with an almost unbearable pain; the girls exchanged excited murmurs in their accepted English, as if X's greedy appetite pleased them; he could hear their voices distinctly but he could not understand their words. It was then that the midnight feast took an abrupt salacious turn, X tried to protest, his dressing gown was torn open, his naked body was exposed, feebly he tried to hide his genitals but the girls snatched his hands away; shouting with glee, the girls hoisted him to their shoulders, his considerable bulk of nearly two hundred pounds, crying "Heave-ho! Here we go." And stumbling and staggering like drunken revelers they bore him flailing and kicking into the sumptuous bedroom, with much laughter and little ceremony he was dropped onto the rumpled bed, which he'd feared was the girls' destination from the first, theirs and his.

When X opened his mouth to protest, for he was a contentedly married man, and a gentleman, a bold kiss stopped it; the acrobatic French girl with her sinewy, squirmy body pinioned him to the mattress, and one of the German girls clambered beside him; the girls had shed their bellboy costumes, and X himself was naked now; he would have cringed in shame except his aged flaccid body was pronounced beautiful by his captors, his skin admiringly stroked, how handsome X was! how manly! The girls took turns straddling his chest, kissing him with deep, sucking kisses; sucking at his tongue as if to tear it from his mouth; sucking at his breath; X could feel, against his strangely cool, dampish skin, the powerful heat of the girls' skin; the heat between their naked thighs as they straddled his chest and belly; the crinkly damp of their pubic hair; the pulse and throb of their young bodies. When had they tied him, wrists and ankles, to the four carved-mahogany posts of the immense canopied bed?—tied him with silken cords? His hairy navel, his hollow, sagging belly-button, was smeared with pâté to be licked by rapacious, tickling tongues; he was being forced to lick goat cheese from the navel of the fleshier of the German girls; all the girls shrieked with impudent laughter; if X's enemies saw him now, what tales they would spread! what legends! The girls were vying with one another to touch, to fondle, to stroke his limp penis, a limp veined old carrot of a penis, and the testicles delicate and cool as quails' eggs; roughly the girls tickled his pubic hair which was a coarse yellow-white, like wires; the German fraulein had discovered the scar from X's abdominal surgery of several years ago, an eight-inch scar like a zipper in his sallow flesh, and playfully she ran manicured red talons up and down the scar—"Zipzipzip, Herr X!" Tonia, or Tanya, panting with desire, had smeared her buoyant breasts with whipped cream, and her pert little nipples were maraschino cherries X was obliged to eat, how she screamed when he bit her, screamed and kicked and struck him with her hard fists, so that for an instant he was terribly afraid. But the French girl was squealing in triumph for she'd managed at last to stroke X's penis into a steely rod, all the girls exclaimed at its length, its elasticity, its healthy burnished-red hue, its throbbing heat; greedily they competed to hold it, to stroke and caress it, to kiss its tip that gleamed with precious juices, the very elixir of life. "Stop. No. Please," X begged. For the sensation was almost more than he could bear. He was covered in perspiration and panting as if he'd run up the seven flights of stairs to this very room. His heart was banging like an impatient fist against his rib cage. One of the girls had lowered herself over his penis, having stroked it to a red-hot rod, and had fitted her satiny, smooth and muscular vagina over it, thrusting herself down upon him, and gripping him tightly; X heard his groans like strangulation; groans like he was sobbing, and then he was laughing; the lights in the bedroom were in fact candle flames and these flames were now being blown out. X pleaded, "Stop! My dignity! Don't you know who I am!" and at once the girls cried, "Yes, we know who you are, you are X, the last man of letters!" And a scalding geyser erupted from the very pit of his belly; his eyes flew open, and his heart ceased beating; the astonishment of such a moment, the wonder of it; he was alive after all, alive, and young, and his life lay before him; the shell that was X slipped away, he was free, triumphant. "Thank you!"—X's words were sobs, a lover's plea, snatched from his throat even as consciousness was extinguished like a blinding-bright fluorescent light in a white-tiled bathroom.

And in the morning they found him. After X failed to respond to telephone calls and anxious knockings at his door. His Italian publisher, who'd arrived to escort X personally to the airport, directed the hotel manager to force the double-locked door; and there in the darkened bedroom lay the old man lifeless on the carpet beside his bed; the bedclothes were in a turmoil, tangled in X's naked limbs; his arms were outflung as if in protest; champagne had been spilled on the carpet, and on X; there was a lurid trace of chocolate on X's gaping mouth, and what appeared to be a pâté smeared on his torso and belly; his face was deathly pale, and his cheeks sunken; his dentures were in a water glass beside his bed. X's eyes were starkly open, yet sightless; the left eyeball was turned up into his head as if peering inside, inquisitively.

High Crime Area

Detroit, Michigan. April 1967.

One of them is following me. I think it must be the same (male, black) figure I've seen in the past. But I could be mistaken.

From the rear entrance of Starret Hall at the edge of the Wayne State University campus, through faculty parking B, along a littered pedestrian walkway that opens onto Cass Avenue —I am aware of this lone figure behind me as you'd be aware of small flames licking at the edge of your vision. Thinking *There is no one. And even if there is someone, I will not look.*

Ascending concrete steps, nearly turning an ankle. Walking too quickly. *Will not look!*

It's 6:25 P.M. Not yet dusk. Not yet, the bright arc lights that illuminate certain near-deserted walkways and corners of the sprawling urban campus.

For days the sky above Detroit has been overcast and wintry. A fine red-ashy haze when shards of sun push through the clouds, from factories in River Rouge. As the sky darkens, the air seems to coarsen. Your eyes and lungs smart, it's a mistake to walk too quickly—in the desolate streets at this edge of the University, a hurrying figure is an alarming sight.

Sudden shouts, screams—you don't want to hear.

Rapidly my brain works: is the (male, black) figuring following a woman who happens to be me; or is the (male, black) figure following *me*?

If it's just a (white, lone) woman who is being followed, I will be able to elude the (male, black) figure—I think. If it's *me* who is being followed, the situation is more serious.

I am prepared, this time: I am *armed*.

In my shoulder bag, a small handgun. Snub-nosed nickel-plated .22-caliber Sterling Arms semiautomatic that weighs more than you'd think, with only a three-inch barrel.

I've just come from teaching a class in composition in Starret Hall.

To my students, I am *Mz. Mc'tyre*. The name usually mispronounced in a mumble as if there is something inherently embarrassing in speaking my name at all.

If *Mz. Mc'tyre* is being followed, that is not so good.

In this class, which is listed as English 101: Composition, there are twenty-nine students formally registered of whom several have not appeared in weeks. There has not been a single class meeting attended by all of the students including even the first meeting when I'd read off their names and tried to determine, by their murmured responses, whether I'd pronounced the names correctly. (At least half of the names were virtually unpronounceable—by me.) For I was a young teacher, in just my second year of part-time teaching at Wayne State, and eager not to offend.

Two months later, I am no longer that young teacher, I think. But I am still in dread of offending.

Like many new teachers, I hope *to be liked*. I hope *to be respected* as well, but will settle for *being liked*.

Yet, I think that I have failed at *being liked*.

I am not a full-time instructor in the English Department, nor even in the College of Liberal Arts. I have an adjunct appointment in the Continuing Education Division—"night school" as it's called, condescendingly. I have a master's degree in English from the University of Michigan, and not a Ph.D. I have published a few stories and poems in small literary journals but I have published only one scholarly article, in *Philological Quarterly*. (No one knows this, but that scholarly article will be my last as it is my first.) And so, though I am negligible among the Wayne State faculty, and beneath the radar of those who control tenure-track appointments, still I am hopeful.

My CE ("Continuing Ed") students are older than the average undergraduate, some of them in their late thirties, forties. Just a few are my age or younger. (I am twenty-six.) The racial proportion of the class is approximately seventy percent individuals "of color"—(predominantly black)—twenty percent individuals "of Asian descent"—(predominantly Chinese)—ten percent "white"—(including recent immigrants from East Europe). On the whole, the Asian students are younger than the others, and so slender, so youthful, so rapt in attention, they might be mistaken for undergraduates, or even high school students; it's awkward that the Asian students are generally more skilled in English than their black classmates born in the United States, though for the Asians, English is a second, recently acquired language.

(Why am I so preoccupied with racial identities, skin "colors"?—-I'd never been, until moving to Detroit, Michigan, with my husband soon after our marriage, and being hired to teach at a state university with a broad social mission—as the joke was, to teach the unteachable who'd attended Detroit public schools.)

But I love my students at Wayne State! I want to love them.

I think they must sense this. I think they must see the yearning in my eyes, that shifts too readily to unease, alarm, and fear; the yearning that is so very close to woundedness and hurt; yet, an expression of determination, *I will make a difference in your lives. Just help me!*

Yes, I would be deeply ashamed. If my students knew that their idealistic teacher has been coming to the Wayne State campus *armed.*

Students in the class who are old enough to be my parents gaze upon me with a curious sort of tenderness, even protectiveness; they smile at my attempts at levity, and nod at virtually everything I say, or write on the blackboard. They are my champions: they like me! One of my few white, male students is a police officer who at the start of the course told me he was obliged to wear his service revolver in our class, beneath his jacket, but that he hoped never to use it—not ever.

What would this husky young man think, if he knew that his instructor Mz. McIntyre has brought a (concealed) handgun with her to class, several times; a handgun for which she has acquired no permit.

For to apply for a permit would be to make my fear public. And I am very ashamed of my fear.

A number of the students seem immune to my efforts at friendliness. They gaze at me skeptically, or resentfully; their dislike sharpens each time I am obliged to hand back their papers, covered in helpful red ink. At times their dislike shades into contempt, or impatience, not so much for who I am, or who they believe I am, a young white woman with a nervously cheerful manner, but because they perceive me as an individual, not coincidentally "white," who stands between them and the next, crucial stage of their lives.

To them, education is a ladder. Their courses are rungs. They are climbing the ladder, a rung at a time. They can't afford to do poorly—to "fail." They can't afford to throw away tuition money. They are part-time students hoping to acquire degrees in such practical subjects as business administration, accounting, education, nursing, radiology, social work; judging by the autobiographical information they've included in their compositions, all have full-time jobs and most have families including "dependents."

In the corridors of Starret Hall, in the rarely cleaned restrooms, female students laugh together, sometimes shriek with laughter—it's disconcerting to hear, especially at a distance, as they seem to be screaming for help. While teaching I'd several times heard female voices in the corridor outside the room, and sudden peals of shrieking laughter, and became so distracted I couldn't remember what I was saying . . . A sensation of horror washed over me. *God forgive me I ignored cries for help. A girl was raped, strangled . . . I pretended not to hear.*

Oily perspiration on my sickly-sallow-"white" face, and students in my classroom gazing at me with polite puzzled faces.

The shrieks have been (only) laughter, evidently. Quickly subsiding, and harmless.

Among the compositions my students have written the most disturbing is one turned in last week in by a young black woman who stares at me in class with blank (insolent?) eyes that fail to register my attempts at mirth or levity, whom I often see in the corridor before our class, laughing with her friends. Vernella is a hospital worker at Detroit General and has expressed a wish to enroll in the School of Nursing—if her grades are high enough. When I pass Vernella in the hall or on the stairs she cuts her eyes at me and mumbles what sounds like *H'lo Mz.*— (name indecipherable)—with a tight twitch of a smile even as her eyes remain narrowed, coolly assessing. Vernella's writing has not improved significantly since the start of the course and with the passage of time she has become increasingly sulky and impatient when others speak or read their compositions aloud.

She sighs often, loudly; she fumbles in her enormous handbag, sometimes for a tissue with which to wipe her caramel-colored face, sometimes for a crinkly little cellophane bag of what appear to be tiny chocolates. Perhaps because she has worked a full day at the hospital before coming to our class—(as Vernella has informed me, more than once)—she leans her chin against her hand, slipping into a light doze. She is one of those whom I've tried to win over, to *liking me,* without success. She appears to be about my age, a solid, fleshy young woman with grease-flattened hair and dark maroon lipstick-lips. Her most recent composition and the one that has disturbed me is a character sketch of her thirty-year-old cousin serving a twenty-five-year sentence for manslaughter at the Slate River Correctional Facility (once known as the Michigan Asylum for Insane Criminals—but that was long ago), who'd converted to "Black Islam" in prison. Vernella writes by hand, on lined tablet paper, carefully and laboriously like a grammar school pupil and so the impact of her words seems to me both childlike and threatening. *Joah be religis to surprise of our fambly, he have his way of speaking that is Black Islam which is beleif that the White Devel is the enemy of all Black People. Joah say the "War" be starting soon in a citty like Detroit where white polis rain agains the Black. Joah say no white persson is worthy of Trust as history from Civil War to know, has reveled, they are all Enemy and will be punisht.*

With my red ballpoint pen like any devoted English teacher I drew faint querying lines beneath *religis, fambly, Devel, citty, polis, rain ("reign"?), agains, persson, punisht* and in the margins of the composition politely I queried *Clear? Transition?* or noted *More development needed* or *Reorganize paragraph for clarity?* I noted *Interesting! Excellent! More examples?* Though barely literate Vernella's writing exuded the uncensored ring of truth.

No subject had inspired Vernella until this one. Everything she'd written previously had been stiff, unconvincing. Here, I could hear the breathless indignation in her words. Between us was the pretext that Vernella had successfully fulfilled an assignment that would require revision to raise it to a grade of C.

Confronted with a number of barely literate student writers at the start of the course I'd decided not to grade them at all, out of a wish not to discourage them. (And not to provoke their animosity. I may have been a new, young, naïve instructor, but I was not a fool.) Instead I handed back the weaker compositions lightly annotated in red ink, and arranged for private conferences with the students so that we could go through their work line by line. Having writers read their work aloud is helpful, if laborious. What emerged from the conferences were compositions that were collaborative efforts, but which I could claim were written by the students themselves. There were a few reliable writers in the class who received grades of B and B+; there was a middle-aged black minister to whom I hoped to give an A- by the end of the course. The young Asian students routinely earned B+, A-, and an occasional A, but no black student had yet written even an A- paper and I knew that they resented this—"racial discrimination."

At each class meeting an ever-shifting number of students failed to hand in assignments, or handed in assignments late; it wasn't unusual for a student who'd missed several classes to return with back assignments and stammered apologies of varying degrees of sincerity. (One of the older students, male, Ukrainian, returned after a month's absence with a shaved head and battered-looking face, walking on crutches, not caring to explain what had happened to him except he'd been "hospitalized" with a head injury.) Repeatedly I'd had to modify my stern warning that late papers would be downgraded—I didn't have the heart to discourage someone who was writing at a C level, with obvious effort; yet, each time I made an exception, I was weakening my authority, melting away like heaps of befouled Detroit snow on the pavement. Nor did I want to fail a student because he or she had missed too many classes, as we were supposed to do, following university policy.

I wanted to give high grades. Badly I wanted not to give failing grades. By this point in the semester it seemed inevitable that at least one-quarter of the class might receive grades below C, and those who'd disappeared from the course were supposed to receive grades of F. Vernella's grades hovered between D and C–; she had not come to see me during office hours, with the excuse that she'd had to work at the hospital, or had problems at home. My heart clutched, thinking of her, and of the animosity in her composition; there was a kind of *faux*-naïve impudence in the very way she regarded me in our classroom, seated at a desk beside a window, fattish thigh of one leg slung over the other, legs shimmering in silver tights and boots to the knee. Her earlobes were pierced with glittery hoops and her fingernails shone with what appeared to be zebra stripes. She sat in front of a tall long-limbed young black man named Razal with a face like something scorched who often leaned forward as if to inhale her stiff lusterless hair. Razal poked Vernella, they whispered and giggled together. At such times, I avoided looking toward Vernella at all.

These were not adolescent high school students but *adults*. This was the Wayne State University Continuing Education Division, not the undergraduate College of Liberal Arts but the "night school"—you would not expect of an instructor in this division that she would have to discipline adult students.

Yet sometimes I saw—(I thought that I saw)—Vernella with the young black Razal—(or someone who resembled Razal)—elsewhere on campus. I would not have wished to concede that, in the myopia of unease, very likely I was confusing my students with strangers who resembled them, for I dared not look at them very closely out of a wish not to force them to greet me, or regard me with "friendly" smiles. Yet, I seemed to see Vernella and Razal often, and couldn't help but notice how their eyes glided over me, deliberately not-seeing me, as if I were invisible—their anxious white-woman instructor with the obscure last name.

I was sure that they waited for me to pass by so that they could murmur and laugh together.

Since the previous Tuesday I'd lain awake in bed beside my (sleeping, oblivious) husband tormenting myself with the character sketch Vernella had written in her large, childish handwriting on the subject of her cousin Joah—*All they beliefs come from the Korran that is Allah word they say. The White Church not to be trust for Jesus was a Black Man like Muhammed so Joah say. I am not in judgement of these for my momma tell us there is Good and Evil in all the racis.*

What absurd gratitude I felt, for Vernella's unnamed mother!

I waited in my office in Starret Hall for Vernella to come to see me as she'd said she would, in the late afternoon, but she hadn't shown up. This had been the third time at least, since the start of the semester, that Vernella hadn't shown up for an appointment. Sitting at my battered aluminum desk pressing my fingers against my throbbing forehead, hoping smirking Vernella wouldn't come. Please please please please *please.* Do not come *please.* No relief so vast as the realization that a "problem" student isn't coming and that you are free to go home earlier than you'd planned.

Or just sit at your desk, feeling depleted as an old tire whose air has leaked out, imperceptibly. No drama, just the slow imperceptible leak. *But I am still young! I am—how old?—twenty-six . . .* With a dazed smile scratching with a fingernail at some sort of mucus-spillage on the aluminum desk top in the shape of a mandala.

Melancholy romance of such settings: classroom buildings in off-hours. Fluorescent-lit corridors, trash bins overflowing,

Styrofoam cups left on windowsills and on stairs. Stale air recycled smelling of cigarette smoke and disinfectant, echo of raised voices and thunderous sounds of feet on stairs. If there is graffiti in such buildings it is graffiti executed solely in off-hours.

Sometimes in the corridor there are footsteps, subdued voices, laughter—abruptly silenced as if cut off by a giant hand.

There may be one security guard in Starret Hall, several floors below and if I called for help, if I screamed, he would not hear. That is why I have brought the "semiautomatic" with me, that I have never (yet) fired.

My body stings with perspiration, at the prospect of even fumbling for this gun in my shoulder bag. Daring to remove it, "display" it. Lift it in my hand, "aim" it—"fire" . . .

I will never do this, I know. I can never do this.

Joah he says he Know what he know. Since incarcceraton Joah be a wiser man and older saying he will never make Mistakes in the White World ever again, when he is releast on parol.

We are three months before the race riot of sweltering July 1967. But no one can know that, in wintry April.

The secret handgun: a purchase from another instructor. A secret from friends as from my unsuspecting students. And my husband.

Drew had given me rudimentary lessons in using the gun. Safety, how to load, what kind of bullets, how to clean. (Not that I planned on cleaning the gun.) How to aim the barrel, how to "gently press" the trigger. Assuring me that I didn't really have to be skilled at using a firearm, all I'd need to do was allow anyone who was threatening me to know that I had one—I was *armed.*

Like me Drew was an adjunct teacher which is to say temporary, expendable and near-anonymous. He had a master's degree in English and "communication skills." Of course, he was *white.*

He was leaving Detroit, he'd said. Moving across the continent to Seattle. He'd given up trying to establish a life here in this city that was paved-over like a great parking lot yet had the feel of shifting-sands, that could fall away beneath your feet and suck you down to Hell.

If I can get to Cass Avenue. And across. And to the parking garage. There is likely to be—well, there might be—someone in or near the parking garage, at this time—another faculty member and so there would be two of us, and only one of *him.*

Frightened white faces, like mine. Snug inside their pockets, worn against their hearts, or hidden in their shoulder bags or briefcases, secret weapons like mine?

Probably not. Possibly.

Would I dare remove it? Would I dare—lift it, aim the barrel, press my terrified finger against the trigger? Shoot another person, even in self-defense?

Drew had said, you don't have to aim it, even. Just reveal it, that would be enough. Fire it into the air. Fire wildly. And scream. Just to demonstrate you aren't defenseless, helpless.

Wildly now I am thinking *I will do this! I am strong enough.*

Here, to my right as I approach Cass Avenue, is the six-foot concrete wall covered in graffiti, that has drawn my eye since the start of the fall term. On this ruin of a wall is a tangle of impassioned scribbles like the art of Miró, Klee, Picasso—not a primitive or crude form of that art but near-identical to it. I inquired about the startling graffiti but no one was very helpful. My questions were met with looks of bemusement, disdain— *Sorry! No idea. It all looks the same to us—ugly.*

Briefly, before other distractions intervened, and the responsibility of teaching remedial English became a sort of obsession, I'd contemplated the possibility of writing an appreciative essay on the graffiti, and taking photographs of the "art." I have to concede, I'd imagined making an impression with an essay of this sort, that might appear in an intellectual literary journal, and draw attention to the (white) (woman) author as well as to the unknown artist . . . But with the passage of months the graffiti has begun to fade into the general shabbiness of the urban campus. The artist hasn't revisited the wall. I want to protest to him—*But you are special. You shouldn't remain anonymous.*

He will remain anonymous. Maybe he isn't even alive any longer.

The mortality rate for young black men in Detroit is said to be nine times higher than that for their white counterparts. Likelihood of incarceration, even higher.

At Cass, I cross the wide, windy avenue as swiftly as I can without breaking into a run or turning an ankle like a fool. Slow-moving traffic on the avenue, city buses, trucks belching diesel exhaust, but mostly sidewalks are deserted at this hour at the scruffy edge of the campus.

Behind me whoever is following me accelerates his pace, crossing Cass against the light on long striding legs.

Calmly I am thinking *It is just a coincidence. This person is not really following me.*

Calmly I am thinking *He can't know that I am armed. As soon as it is revealed, in whatever way it will be revealed, he will disappear.*

I would not have to fire the gun, I was sure. I would not have to kill another person.

Yet my heartbeat has quickened. Almost, I'm unable to breathe.

Not panic. A reasonable apprehension, in this place and at this time.

Sweat breaking out beneath my clothes which are the remnants of winter wear—dark-crimson down coat with a hood, black woolen trousers, knit gloves. For weeks in March the temperature seemed frozen—literally—at 32°F; only grudgingly has the air turned warmer.

The last time I'd been followed off campus whoever had been following me seemed to become discouraged when, on Cass, a city bus wheezed to a stop to disgorge passengers with whom I mingled like a clumsy white goose among dark-feathered Canada geese—what relief! I'd almost laughed, I was so elated. And when I'd glanced back, the (male, black) figure seemed to have vanished.

Ninety percent of muggings, rapes, even homicides in Detroit are what the police label *opportunistic*. Meaning the victim happened to be in the wrong place at the wrong time. *Bad luck. Nothing personal.*

But this evening there's no bus. At least, no bus that's going to stop. And there's no one on this stretch of pavement except me, conspicuous in my pale skin as a mollusk shorn of its shell.

White Devel. Enemy Black People.

My husband had said, You don't have to teach there. You don't have to teach at all.

I'd said, But—I do.

He said, Look. You *don't*.

It was true: my husband had a good job and could support us both. Some measure of old-fashioned pride lay lodged deep within him. *A man should support his wife. A man should not allow his wife to work in demeaning or dangerous circumstances.*

Wayne State is in a high crime area, my husband said. He'd meant to be kindly and not bullying.

High crime area was an expression commonly heard in the media, seen in print. As commonplace in Detroit and vicinity as the parallel expression *exclusive suburb Grosse Pointe.*

What is the proportion of black and white citizens who are *armed*?

Recently it was revealed that there are at least two firearms for each citizen of Detroit though in the same news article it was acknowledged that this was a figure compiled from gun registrations only. Many more "firearms" are not registered as they are illegal purchases and of these, many are in the possession of individuals under twenty-one.

Crime in Detroit is "predominantly black"—and yet, victims-of-crime in Detroit are "predominantly black." White citizens have fled and are fleeing to "white suburbs."

But we have not yet fled. We are stubborn, or guileless. We are not yet ready to make the leap.

The (male, black) figure is approximately twenty feet behind me. He isn't gaining on me—he has slowed his pace since running across the street. I can hear something—whistling? Humming? *Is he singing under his breath?*

Dark skin. Young, lean, and edgy like a boxer who's too tall for his weight, and his arms and legs too long. No jacket, bare muscled arms, denim cap pulled low over his forehead.

He's a stranger—I think. He is no one I know.

No one who should know *me*.

We are headed east on that short, narrow street off Cass. Suddenly it seems to be dusk—the red-hazy air has darkened. I'm walking swiftly in the awkward way in which people walk when they believe they're being followed but don't want the follower to know that they're aware of being followed—head slightly ducked, shoulders stiff, arms tight against my sides. My veins are flooded with adrenaline like hot acid and I feel a kind of crazy elation—wanting to break into a run. But I know that this would be a mistake. *He will know, then. It will be acknowledged between us.*

How exposed I am feeling, a (lone, white) woman. At the same time trying to console myself—*He's a student. He's from the University. He doesn't want to hurt me.*

If he could see me now my husband would chide—Why did you stay so late in that building, who did you imagine you were waiting for?

Furious chiding me—What are you trying to prove? That you don't need a marriage, you don't need *me*?

Ahead is the parking garage. Five floors, near-empty, my car on the third level. I can't step inside, into that dark interior. In my panic I think—*Should I run? But where?*

Should I fumble in my shoulder bag and reveal it—the illegal, terrifying pistol?

Once I have done this I will have crossed over, I am thinking. All that is secret will be revealed. And if I "fire" the gun—my life will be changed, irrevocably.

I know this. This is inescapable.

I am panting, sweating. A roaring in my ears like a great cataract.

And then, I've made a decision: I have turned to the man who has been tormenting me, and I am holding my shoulder bag in such a way that I can reach inside, if required; and I will not hesitate, if required.

I am trembling badly but my voice is stronger than I'd expected. I am saying, "Excuse me! Are you—do you—want something?"

My question seems to have taken the man by surprise.

"Ma'am? What you sayin?"

He has no idea how desperate I am. No idea what I am carrying in my shoulder bag. I am not the type, he has been thinking.

But whatever he's been expecting, he has not expected me to turn and confront him.

Of course, I am very nervous. I am trying not to stammer.

"I'm asking—are you following me? Why are you following me?"

"Ma'am! Not following anybody."

Wariness in his eyes, that are large, and hooded. And a kind of bemusement. His lips draw back in a wary smile.

"But I think you are. I think you've been—following me. You've been following me since . . ."

Now that I can see the man's face, I realize that he's a former student of mine, from the first semester I'd taught at Wayne State. But it isn't clear if he remembers *me*.

His name is—Ezra? Ezekiel? His last name, I can't recall.

Ezekiel had been the first "casualty" among my students—as I'd thought at the time. The first of my Wayne State students to disappear with no explanation from a class of mine.

Because he'd dropped out of the course without securing permission from the University, I'd had to give Ezekiel a grade of F. I'd have given him an I ("Incomplete") if he'd requested it, but he had not requested it. Ezekiel's attendance in the course had been sporadic and unpredictable and in class he'd shifted almost continually, maddeningly in his seat beside a steam radiator, legs too long for the desk, head lifted at an odd angle as if, beneath my voice, or drowning out my voice, he was hearing another, more crucial interior voice, or an intoxicating interior music. Often Ezekiel's face crinkled in frowns, grimaces. He smiled, but not at me. His eccentric behavior seemed to disconcert some of the other, more subdued students, but except for his occasional blunt stare he'd never seemed threatening to me or to anyone. I had not quite dared to call on him, but a few times he'd lifted his hand to answer a question of mine, with the demeanor of a schoolboy.

The fact was, I'd felt a tinge of loss when Ezekiel disappeared from my class. There's no rebuke to an instructor quite like an empty, abandoned desk in a classroom. No more clear sign of failure.

Now, I am hesitant to utter Ezekiel's name, for fear that I have remembered it wrongly. I don't want to insult him, confusing him with another (black, male) student.

Maybe, I have remembered him wrongly.

Ezekiel has thrust his hands deep into his pockets as if to force me to see, he isn't dangerous. His trousers are tight, no room for any handgun though there might be room for a slender knife or a razor—I am thinking.

There is something impudent about this handsome young black man's bemused drawl: "Maa'aam? Maybe I was followin you, seein it was you." He laughs, loudly. "Thinkin it was you, Mz. Mc'tyre."

So he remembers my name. He remembers *me*.

Yet, until this moment it hasn't been clear if he'd known who I was. Like me, he hadn't remembered. And he mumbles my name as if enunciating it clearly would suggest an awkward intimacy between us.

We are standing on the sidewalk near the front entrance of the parking garage. There is less than ten feet between us. In my extreme unease I'm hardly able to speak, nor even compose my face. Should I be smiling in recognition of Ezekiel, or in relief? Should I be as wary as before? *Should I be frightened?*

Ezekiel removes one of his hands from his pocket, to stroke his jaws that are covered in short bristly hairs. Until this moment, I hadn't noticed that he has a beard, a goatee. (But Ezekiel hadn't had a beard when he was in my class, had he? I was sure he had not.) Though he wants to suggest that he's in supreme control of the situation, Ezekiel is still surprised by my turning to confront him—the last thing he'd expected was this white, lone woman turning to him, to challenge him, in this desolate place.

He is eyeing my shoulder bag. I think I see this. Eyeing my large bulky quasi-leather shoulder bag in which I carry a paperback textbook and student papers but also car keys and a wallet. Money, credit card. Not much money, but Ezekiel could not know that.

And the heavy little handgun. Ezekiel could not know.

Rapidly my mind works—has Ezekiel been planning to follow me into the garage, though it's clear that he has no reason to enter the garage, and announcing then that he has been purposefully following me; has he been following a solitary woman he didn't recognize as a former instructor of his; and with what intent?

With a bright glistening grin Ezekiel asks, as if we've just run into each other casually on the sidewalk: "What you doin here, ma'am? You teachin?"

I tell him *yes*. Briefly, with a small smile *yes*.

Ezekiel is older than I remember, in his early thirties perhaps. Is it ominous, in this chilly weather Ezekiel is wearing
a soiled gray sweatshirt with the sleeves cut crudely off at the
shoulder, as if to display his tight-muscled arms? I can see veins
in his biceps, veins in his forehead. He seems to be perspir-
ing: oozing oily beads of sweat, as in a drug high. *Is he high
on drugs? Is he deranged?* A wave of dread comes over me, one
of Ezekiel's hands remains inside his trouser pocket . . . He is
fondling the edge of a knife blade, is he?—or, with equal sur-
reptitiousness, the edge of his genitals. *Is he touching himself?
Defiantly, in front of me?*

I am staring at Ezekiel's face. I am (resolutely) not looking at
his hand slow-moving inside his trousers. Yet, the terror comes
over me, obviously Ezekiel has a knife, Ezekiel would not be
without a weapon in the inner city of Detroit if but to defend
himself, and if Ezekiel has a knife, he is now drawing his forefinger over the blade, caressing, calibrating its sharpness; he is
imagining how he will use this blade, how he will use both hands
(of course) seizing my hair, yanking me forward, and down,
down on my knees, deftly he will position me so that he can
bring the knife blade swiftly across my throat, and with enough
force to sever the skin, the tissue, cartilage, a vein, the throbbing carotid artery—this will not be a frenzied slaughter—(I
think)—but something like an execution. And very swiftly and
deftly executed, for it has been planned and, for all I know, it
has already been executed. It has been *memorized*.

The fallen woman, suddenly limp, inconsequential on the filthy pavement. Terrified eyes now blank. Mouth open, but no sound emerges—she is mute, her speech has been taken from her. Possibly she has tried to press her fingers against her throat—to apply pressure to the exploding artery. But she has bled out within minutes. All this has happened already, it is foretold. Beneath the back-flung head, a perfect pool of blood.

Even with the gun, this could happen to me. There is no way I could get the gun out of my shoulder bag, back off and begin to fire—Ezekiel is too quick-witted, and possibly, he is too practiced at wielding a knife.

Yet, numbly I hear myself say: "Yes. I'm teaching the same class—composition. In the same building, I think the same classroom. At the same time, Tuesdays and Thursdays."

Ezekiel, who has been gazing at me with rapt attention, as if seeing something in my face of which I am unaware, doesn't seem to have heard this. He's making a murmurous sound *Uh— yeh?—uh-huh! OK maa'aam!*

Yet, at such a time the bizarre thought comes to me, what it would be like to call such a person *brother*.

Ezekiel, my brother. Ezekiel—is that your name?

As if he has sensed my terror Ezekiel begins to speak rapidly, with a bright damp-toothed smile. He is trying to explain to me—something—that isn't altogether coherent. Such speech is a way of placating terror—as an adult might address a frightened child while advancing upon the child holding something behind his back, or secreted in a pocket. Half-consciously, I step back. Between us there is the pretext that this is a normal conversation, a friendly conversation; the pretext that I'm able to understand him without difficulty, for I am nodding and smiling as teachers invariably do with students, to show sympathy, and to encourage; here is a (female, white) instructor, a (male, black) student near the campus of a sprawling urban university with a mission to educate all citizens. Yes, it is a reversal, a tacit insult: the instructor is younger than the student. This seems wrong. This seems unjust. Perhaps it is "racist." Yet, it is unavoidable. I can't apologize for the person I am, as I can't apologize for the myriad circumstances that have brought me here, or for the (conspicuous) color of my skin. And I am now recalling, prompted by something Ezekiel says, how at the end of the last class he'd attended he'd told me that he had to *go inside* for a while and didn't think he could finish the course. In shame he'd lowered his voice so that I could hardly hear him. So that others standing nearby couldn't hear him. At the time I had no idea what he meant but later, hearing a night school colleague speak wonderingly of a student who'd actually been arrested in a classroom in Starret Hall, led out of the room handcuffed by two uniformed police officers, I realized that Ezekiel must have meant that he was *going inside* what was called, somewhat euphemistically, a "correctional facility"—he'd been, to use the familiar Detroit term, "incarcerated."

No one *went to prison*. Criminals were *incarcerated*.

Whatever Ezekiel's crime, it couldn't have been very serious. Or he'd been allowed to plead guilty to a lesser charge. The sentence couldn't have been long. (Was Ezekiel paroled? Had something happened, he'd been *released*?) For now Ezekiel is standing before me, his former English teacher, smiling and smirking, not certain what he seems to be telling me, or what his intentions are.

Still, he is tracing the outline of the knife inside his trousers. He isn't carrying a gun, there isn't room for even a small gun inside those trousers. He isn't touching his genitals—I am sure, it's a knife blade. Above and to the left of his groin. A slender knife would fit there, as a handgun would not. His bluish-lidded eyes half-close, his fleshy lips retain a dreamy smile. *He is imagining it: the swift deep cut. The explosion of blood that is not "white" but a dark, satisfying red.* Yet, in a resolutely calm and friendly voice I am asking Ezekiel if he's taking courses this semester at Wayne State and he shrugs enigmatically—maybe yes, maybe no. (The question has flattered him, I think. It is also unexpected. It is causing Ezekiel to rapidly reassess the situation—and himself.)

Overhead, the sky is streaked with red, splotched like fraying clouds. The air smells of chemicals, diesel exhaust. I wonder if I should compliment Ezekiel on his muscled arms—*Do you work out, Ezekiel? In a gym?*—but the thought comes to me that this is too familiar, too intimate, and probably Ezekiel would have to say he's been working out in prison.

That is, a correctional facility.

And I might ask him, blindly, daringly—*Is this Slate River? Do you know an inmate approximately your age there, a black*

Muslim, his name is—Joah? The cousin of one of my students this semester . . .

Ezekiel's bluish-dreamy hooded eyes blink slowly. Pointedly, Ezekiel glances around. No one on the street. No one inside the parking garage. Yet, a half-block away at Cass, there is a stream of traffic. And now, streetlights have come on, as if grudgingly. At any moment, a Detroit police cruiser might turn onto this narrow side street and drive slowly past us. At any moment, two (white) police officers in the cruiser, clearly visible beneath the windshield. More than once I'd felt myself saved from similar ambiguous situations in Detroit, an empty stretch of sidewalk, lone individuals or teenagers behind me suddenly very quiet, and then—the police cruiser . . . Though afterward recounting the experience to colleagues and friends—(not ever to my husband!)—I'd underplayed my vast heart-stopping relief, and ridiculed my fears.

As if he's made a decision, as if (perhaps) he understands perfectly all that has rushed through my mind, Ezekiel says in an oddly elevated voice, as if he hopes to be overheard by witnesses, "Maa'aam, I'm gon walk with you, you look like you need somebody walkin with you."

He removes his hand from his pocket. Like an overgrown boy he adjusts the cap more securely on his head.

Walk with me—where?

Quickly I tell Ezekiel that I'm going to the library, to meet my husband. I am not going to the parking garage after all.

Ezekiel smiles, hearing this. He's amused, he knows that I am inventing, out of desperation; such invention is natural to him, and he admires it, in me.

I tell Ezekiel that I don't need him to walk with me. I thank Ezekiel but repeat, I don't need him to walk with me.

Ezekiel frowns happily, shaking his head. "Ma'am, I goin to the lib'ry too, infact. That's where I'm goin, we c'n walk together."

"But—"

"Ma'am, we goin there. Over that way, in't it?"

And so my decision is made for me: I will not need to fumble in my shoulder bag. I will not need to reveal the gun shaking in my (white) hand. I will not need to (blindly) fire at Ezekiel staring at me in quick-dawning horror. I will not need to cross over into that other life.

I am relieved—am I? I am numb.

And numbly then setting out in the direction of the university library, with my former student. And neither of us has been revealed to the other. And neither of us has been exposed to the other. Now I see the name of the short, dark block: Trumbell. Ezekiel is protective of me, even chiding—"Ma'am, crossin this street, better watch out." As if the gesture is altogether natural, Ezekiel dares to take my arm—closes his strong fingers about my arm, above the elbow. The gesture seems to be unpremeditated and curiously impersonal but I am sweating profusely now and fear that I will smell of my body.

"Ma'am, watch out for them fuckin potholes . . ."

Fuckin. It is a rude little nudge, this word. Ezekiel speaking to his former instructor in a way to convey both concern and sexual disrespect.

Once across Cass we make our way onto the near-deserted campus. We are a strange couple—you would glance at us curiously, and perhaps you would stare after us—*Who are they? Not lovers—are they? Will one turn upon the other, to inflict harm? To murder?* We pass a graffiti-covered wall but it is undistinguished, uninspired graffiti—not graffiti to which I would wish to call Ezekiel's attention. And passing a row of darkened wood-frame houses, remnants of a residential neighborhood, renovated, with "modern" facades—CAMPUS MINISTRY. THIRD WORLD CENTER. PSYCHOLOGICAL COUNSELING. AFRICAN-AMERICAN HOUSE.

Tall arc lights illuminate this central part of the campus. Here, it isn't quite so deserted. Ezekiel is saying that he "go to the lib'ry" every night at this time. Ezekiel insists upon escorting me into the dour granite building, up the steps and inside, where there is a blast of overwarm air, and a security guard seated at a turnstile checking IDs. Here, Ezekiel holds back. And I hesitate.

The guard is a middle-aged black man. He is wearing a uniform, and it appears that he is also wearing a holster and a firearm. "Ma'am?" he says. "You comin in the library?" He has recognized me as a university person—graduate student, younger teacher. He is aware of but has scarcely glanced at Ezekiel hovering a few feet behind me.

Seeing that I'm agitated, though making an effort to appear calm. My tremulous lips, dilated eyes. Clammy-pale skin.

Gripping the unwieldy leather bag in both hands. I will need to retrieve my wallet from the bag, will need to rummage desperately in the bag to find the wallet, for there are other items in the bag including, in a compartment, the bulky little gun which is a secret, and which no one must know about; and from the wallet I will need to extract the laminated plastic ID card with my wanly smiling miniature face, but these complicated maneuvers are much for me to grasp at the moment. Barely I can hear the security guard's voice through the roaring in my ears.

"Ma'am? Somethin wrong?"

Something wrong? At first the question seems to baffle me.

"No. I'm meeting my husband here. Inside—here."

My voice is cracked. My throat is very dry. The gravely frowning security guard cups his hand to his ear, to hear more clearly this barely audible guilty-sounding reply.

When I turn, Ezekiel has vanished. As if he has never been.

Acknowledgments

To the editors of these publications, thank you for originally publishing these stories, several of which have been considerably revised: "The Home at Craigmillnar," *Kenyon Review;* "High," *The Marijuana Chronicles,* ed. Jonathan Santlofer; "Toad-Baby," *Boulevard;* "Demon," *Demon & Other Tales* (Necronomicon Press); "Lorelei," (originally titled "Subway"), *The Dark,* ed. Ellen Datlow; "The Last Man of Letters," *Playboy;* "The Rescuer," *EccoSolo,* "High Crime Area," *Boulevard.*